"A Celibate Marriage?"
Tom Asked.

Kate sniffed and pulled her dress over her head. Wriggling into it, she shook her hair back from her face and stared at him. "At first, Tom, yes."

"At first?" He clung to those two words like a drowning man snatching at a piece of driftwood.

"I just think it would be best if we didn't sleep together right away. If we took our time."

He cocked his head and looked at her through wary eyes. "How much time?"

"I don't know. However long it takes for us to get to know each other. Become friends."

A snort of laughter shot from his lungs. "Friends..."

"What's wrong with that?" she asked, glaring at him.

"Kate," Tom said, giving her a slow up-and-down look. "I've got lots of friends, and not one of them makes me want to strip them naked and carry them off to the forest primeval."

Dear Reader,

April brings showers, and this month Silhouette Desire wants to shower you with six new, passionate love stories!

Cait London's popular Blaylock family returns in our April MAN OF THE MONTH title, *Blaylock's Bride*. Honorable Roman Blaylock grapples with a secret that puts him in a conflict between confiding in the woman he loves and fulfilling a last wish.

The provocative series FORTUNE'S CHILDREN: THE BRIDES continues with Leanne Banks's *The Secretary and the Millionaire*, when a wealthy CEO turns to his assistant for help in caring for his little girl.

Beverly Barton's next tale in her 3 BABIES FOR 3 BROTHERS miniseries, *His Woman, His Child*, shows a rugged heartbreaker transformed by the heroine's pregnancy. Powerful sheikhs abound in *Sheikh's Ransom*, the Desire debut title of Alexandra Sellers's dramatic new series, SONS OF THE DESERT. A marine gets a second chance at love in *Colonel Daddy*, continuing Maureen Child's popular series BACHELOR BATTALION. And in Christy Lockhart's *Let's Have a Baby!*, our BACHELORS AND BABIES selection, the hero must dissuade the heroine from going to a sperm bank and convince her to let *him* father her child—the old-fashioned way!

Allow Silhouette Desire to give you the ultimate indulgence—all six of these fabulous April romance books!

Enjoy!

Joan Marlow Golan
Senior Editor, Silhouette Desire

Please address questions and book requests to:
Silhouette Reader Service
U.S.: 3010 Walden Ave., P.O. Box 1325, Buffalo, NY 14269
Canadian: P.O. Box 609, Fort Erie, Ont. L2A 5X3

COLONEL DADDY
MAUREEN CHILD

SILHOUETTE *Desire*

Published by Silhouette Books

America's Publisher of Contemporary Romance

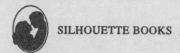

SILHOUETTE BOOKS

ISBN 0-373-76211-9

COLONEL DADDY

This edition published by arrangement with Harlequin Books S.A.

® and TM are trademarks of Harlequin Books S.A., used under license. Trademarks indicated with ® are registered in the United States Patent and Trademark Office, the Canadian Trade Marks Office and in other countries.

Printed in U.S.A.

Books by Maureen Child

Silhouette Desire

Have Bride, Need Groom #1059
The Surprise Christmas Bride #1112
Maternity Bride #1138
*The Littlest Marine #1167
*The Non-Commissioned Baby #1174
*The Oldest Living Married Virgin #1180
*Colonel Daddy #1211

*Bachelor Battalion

MAUREEN CHILD

was born and raised in Southern California and is the only person she knows who longs for an occasional change of season. She is delighted to be writing for Silhouette Books, and is especially excited to be a part of the Desire line.

An avid reader, she looks forward to those rare rainy California days when she can curl up and sink into a good book. Or two. When she isn't busy writing, she and her husband of twenty-five years like to travel, leaving their two grown children in charge of the neurotic golden retriever who is the *real* head of the household. Maureen is also an award-winning historical writer under the names Kathleen Kane and Ann Carberry.

To my editor, Karen Taylor Richman,
for her support and her belief in me.
Thanks for everything, Karen.

One

"Major Jennings to see you, sir," the young corporal said over the intercom.

Colonel Tom Candello pushed a button and said, "Send her in."

He sat back in his chair, his gaze locked on the door across from him. Major Katherine Jennings. Kate. Instantly his mind filled with erotic images. Memories of their last R and R together.

A week in Japan and they'd hardly left the hotel. But it had been like that between them since they'd first met in Hawaii three years ago. A week-long, incredible affair had led to them deciding to meet again the following year. And then the year after. It was always the same. They arranged their leave time to coincide, met at an agreed-upon location, and surrendered to the overwhelming passion they'd found in each other.

And except for that one week a year, they led separate lives. Each of them were career Marines, but they were posted at different bases, thousands of miles from each other, which kept them from ever crossing paths.

Until recently.

Two months ago, Kate had been transferred to Camp Pendleton, California. His base. His command. Now she was not only his once-a-year lover, she was one of his officers. He'd hardly seen her since she arrived. But for one or two brief meetings, where they were surrounded by other Marines, he hadn't really spoken to her since their last morning in Japan.

He stood up abruptly, pushed one hand through his short, black hair and walked to the window. Staring out at the base, he told himself to get rid of the mental images he carried of Kate, naked in bed, her arms held up to welcome him. This wasn't Japan. This wasn't even R and R. This was work, and their two worlds were about to collide.

He felt as though he was on a speeding train heading for a cliff. The brakes were out, and there was no stopping the disaster looming just ahead. All he could do was hang on and wait for it.

A knock at the door brought him out of his thoughts. He turned around, pulled in a deep breath and raced over the edge of the precipice. "Come in."

The door swung open, she stepped inside and quietly closed the door behind her. Then she was there. Standing in his office.

At attention.

"Good afternoon, Colonel," she said stiffly, her right hand slanted in a perfect salute.

"Major," he said and returned her salute, despite feeling a bit awkward about saluting a woman whose body he had explored intimately, thoroughly. "At ease."

She relaxed instantly and his gaze swept over her. Dark green, brimmed cap settled firmly on her head, her short blond hair curled under to lie just along her jawline. Her khaki uniform blouse was starched and ironed to perfection, and a row of ribbons and commendations lay just atop her left breast. Her slim, straight dark skirt stopped just above her knees and she wore regulation high heels that did amazing things for her legs.

He lifted his gaze to her face before he could torture himself further with memories of those legs wrapped around him, holding his body within her tight, damp heat. Damn, this was *not* going to be easy.

Clearing his throat, Tom spoke up. "Kate, it's good to see you." The understatement of the century, he thought, and tried to will his hardened body into submission.

"Thomas," she started and he had to smile. She was the only person he knew who always called him Thomas.

He took a step toward her, but she backed up and held out one hand toward him, palm up, to stop him. "Thomas, we have to talk."

"Yeah," he agreed, knowing she was right to keep her distance. Ever since the day they'd met, there had been fireworks between them. Distance was their only hope. "We do. Kate, we can work with this situation," Tom said. "We're both professionals. Our private time together doesn't have to intrude on our careers."

She took off her hat, tossed it onto a nearby chair, then ran her fingers through her hair. He thought he detected a glimmer of a wry grin before her expression evened out again.

"I'm afraid that ship has sailed, Thomas," she told him softly.

"What are you talking about?" he asked, not really sure he wanted to hear the answer.

"Do you remember that last night in Japan?" she asked, gripping her hands in front of her waist so tightly her knuckles turned white.

Remember it? he wanted to say. The memories still kept him awake at night, his body hard, his mind filled with thoughts of her. They'd toasted each other over a bottle of champagne and spent an hour deciding where they would meet the following year, finally settling on Copenhagen. Then they'd gone out to the balcony of their ridiculously expensive hotel suite and made love under the stars for hours. The memories were so fresh, so ingrained on his mind, Thomas could almost smell the sea air, taste the champagne he'd dribbled onto her nipples and then licked off as she writhed beneath him, moaning his name.

He groaned silently as his body tightened uncomfortably. Aloud, he said only, "Yeah. I remember."

His gaze locked on her face, he saw that she, too, was recalling that night. And if he didn't know better, he'd swear that Major Kate Jennings was blushing. But Kate didn't have an inhibited bone in her gorgeous body, so that couldn't be right.

As their gazes met and held, he began to feel the first twinges of misgiving. She didn't look like a woman who'd just dropped in on her lover for a little stroll down memory lane. "What's this about, Kate?" he asked quietly. "What's wrong?"

As he watched, her pale complexion went shades lighter. Not a good sign. She sucked in a gulp of air like a drowning woman, then blurted, "I'm pregnant, Thomas."

Was that an earthquake?

Tom would have sworn the room had just trembled around him. He shook his head and flicked an uneasy glance at the framed picture of the President, hanging on the wall nearest him. Nope. The picture wasn't swaying. There was no loud, trainlike rumble of sound.

So. It wasn't the earth shaking.

It was him.

Katherine stared at him and watched several different expressions slide across his features. Stunned shock. Disbelief. Anxiety. And finally, acceptance. She recognized all of them. Hadn't she seen the very same expressions staring back at her in the mirror only a month ago?

She hadn't wanted to believe that early pregnancy test kit. At the time, she had still been so stressed from being transferred to Thomas's base, she'd assumed that stress was messing up her cycle. After all, it wasn't going to be easy to face her new commanding officer when that officer had seen her naked. So naturally, she'd bought a few more kits, hoping for a different result. But as she'd stared down at the four little test wands, each of them with a neatly stamped plus sign staring back at her, Kate had had to accept the truth.

She was single, thirty-two years old, a major in the Marines and pregnant for the first time.

Now, after living with the secret for a month, she waited to hear her lover's reaction.

"How did this happen?" he said, almost to himself.

Her eyebrows lifted as she looked at him. "You said you remembered the balcony."

"I do."

"Then you also remember how neither of us wanted to get up and go inside for another condom."

He rubbed one hand across his face as that one defining moment reared up in his mind. "Oh, yeah."

"Yeah." Unable to stand still another moment, Kate started pacing. Her high heels clicked against the linoleum floor, sounding like a rapidfire heartbeat.

Strange, she'd thought the burden of this secret would be lightened by sharing it. But nothing had changed. She was still facing a situation she had no idea how to handle.

And added to that, she couldn't help worrying about what Thomas would say when he recovered from the initial shock.

Her career, her *life*, hung in the balance and seemed to be resting precariously on a tipped pair of scales. She'd spent nearly fourteen years in the Corps, building a career and a reputation to be proud of. It was all she knew. All she'd ever wanted.

All she had.

Now, that was all threatened. A pregnant, married Marine was acceptable. A pregnant unmarried Marine—particularly an officer—could find herself discharged. Or at the very least disgraced and her exemplary career in ruins. At that thought, Kate winced. If she lost the Corps, she wouldn't know what to do with herself.

Hell. She wouldn't even know who she was.

"Kate," Tom said from across the room, "don't work yourself up like this. We'll figure something out."

She stopped short suddenly and swiveled her head to look at him. One thing she had to make perfectly clear right from the beginning. "You should know, Thomas. Ending this pregnancy is *not* an option."

He nodded and gave her a small smile. "I understand."

"I'm not sure I do," she countered and started pacing again. She had never given much thought to social issues. Especially the ones that didn't concern her directly. She'd always been too focused on her career for that. But even Kate had been surprised at the strong, protective instinct that had swelled within her at the discovery of her pregnancy. "I'm a career woman, Thomas. And a firm believer in the ERA. Frankly, I didn't think I'd feel like this. And I can't tell other women what decisions to make about their lives. But for me, I've discovered that there is no decision to make. This baby is a fact. One that we have to deal with. One that isn't going away.''

''Good.''

She stopped again, turning her head to look at him. ''Good?''

He nodded and moved toward her. ''I'm glad you feel that way, Kate. We can handle this. We'll think of something.''

''We will, huh?'' she said, and started pacing again. The sound of her heels on tile echoed on and on in her mind. So stupid. So…irresponsible. How could they have let this happen? They weren't teenagers. They were supposed to be mature adults. *Marines* for God's sake! Her stomach churned uneasily. ''Think, you said?'' she shook her head. ''I hope you have better luck than I've had.'' She paced right up to the wall and turned for the return trip. Glancing into his dark chocolate eyes, she added, ''I've known about this for a month now and I haven't been able to think of a blasted thing.''

''A month?'' he asked. ''Why didn't you tell me sooner?''

''It's not the easiest thing in the world to tell a man, you know,'' she snapped, then caught herself. Sarcasm wasn't going to be a big help here. Throwing her hands up only to let them fall again, she said. ''I needed time. To think. To…'' pretend it wasn't happening? she asked silently as her words trailed off.

''Do you want to leave the Corps?'' he asked quietly.

''No!'' Kate stopped dead, frozen in her tracks. Then she faced him. ''Leave the Corps?'' she repeated, as if she hadn't heard him correctly. "I can't resign. The Corps is my *life*. As much as it is yours. I can't—no. I *won't* give it up."

Did her voice really sound that shrill? Or was it just her?

"Well, then," Thomas said. "That makes things even simpler."

"I don't see how."

His gaze locked with hers. "You know the regulations on pregnancy as well as I do."

A short breath shot into her lungs and caught. "I know." Of course she knew. Wasn't that what had been driving her quietly insane for the last month? Wasn't that why she was wearing a path in his linoleum? Wasn't that why she felt like *crying*, for goodness' sake?

Another long minute passed in silence. Finally Thomas said, "Then you know what the answer to all this is."

She held her breath again and absently wondered if all of this breath holding would hurt a baby currently no bigger than a peanut.

"I would be honored if you would consent to marry me, Kate."

That pent-up breath exploded from her in a rush. Even though she had half suspected he would do exactly this, she was still almost shocked to hear the words out loud.

Marriage.

She should be happy, damn it.

Over the past three years, she'd secretly clung to the hope that one day, he would propose to her. Of course, she had also hoped that a little thing like *love* would prompt his proposal. Instead, it was duty and responsibility guiding the oh-so-honorable man in front of her.

No orange blossoms, candlelight and soft music for them, she mused. Nope. Marine green and Duty.

Lord, how romantic.

She lifted one hand and rubbed at a spot between her eyes, hoping to ease the throbbing headache centered there.

It didn't help.

Kate knew he was right. Their getting married was the only possible solution. But her heart cringed at the notion of a dutiful marriage.

How strange. She'd managed to avoid marriage and motherhood all of her adult life. Now suddenly she was jumping feet first into both.

"Kate?" Tom asked, watching as her expressive face displayed each of her emotions in turn. "This is the best way. The *only* way."

She nodded stiffly, but he could see she wasn't convinced.

"Kate, this can work," he said, walking across the room to her side. Hands on her shoulders, he held her gently but firmly, ignoring the sudden, white-hot jolt of desire that shot through him like a mortar blast. If she accepted his proposal, there would be plenty of time to indulge in the passion they shared. "We like each other. We get along well."

"Like," she repeated numbly and crossed her arms in front of her before letting her gaze slide from his.

He cupped her face in his palm and turned her back

to look at him. "This *will* work," he repeated, warming to his theme. Sure, he'd never intended to get married again. One failure in that department had been more than enough for Tom Candello. And here was another chance to show the world what lousy fathers the Candello men made. Like his own dad before him, Tom had failed at fatherhood. And the thought of another failure wasn't a pretty one. But this was a special circumstance. Kate was pregnant. With *his* baby. Their child. He couldn't let her down.

She needed him.

And for now, that was enough.

On that thought, he suggested, "Think about this as if it's a Corps assignment, Kate."

"What?"

"We're fellow officers. We like each other. We understand each other's work."

She smiled sadly. "Not much to base a marriage on, Thomas."

"More than some people have," he said, and smoothed her hair back behind her ear.

"And less than others."

He knew what she was talking about. Love. Well, love wasn't something he was interested in. Desire at least was honest. And he *did* desire her. Plus he genuinely liked her. Wasn't that better than some indefinable emotion that broke as many hearts as it healed?

Stroking her cheekbone with the pad of his thumb, he said quietly, "Love's not all it's cracked up to be, Kate. I believe we can have a better-than-average marriage just by keeping love out of it. We'll still manage to raise our child in a happy enough environment.''

Kate stared up at him for a long, thoughtful moment. The knot in her throat seemed to grow to colossal proportions, threatening to choke off her air entirely. His words keep repeating themselves over and over in her mind, like a tape stuck on Playback. ''Keep love out of it. Happy enough environment. Better than average marriage.''

Not at all what she'd secretly yearned for the moment she'd first laid eyes on Colonel Thomas Candello. But fantasies and dreams had to give way to the realities of life…didn't they?

And the cold, harsh reality was…she was pregnant. She was a Marine. And without the Corps she would have nothing to offer either herself *or* her child.

Because she really did have no choice at all here, she finally said, ''All right, Thomas. I will marry you.''

He let out a pent-up breath and pulled her to him. As he wrapped his arms around her, Kate let herself lean against him, drawing on the strength he was offering her. Hoping they were doing the right thing.

For the baby *and* for them.

All she knew for sure was that the man she loved was marrying her—not because he couldn't live without her—but because of a baby neither of them had counted on.

Two

"Now that that's settled," he whispered against the top of her head, "how about dinner tonight? We can talk about the specifics."

Kate pulled back from him, despite the reluctance to leave the circle of his arms. Staring up into those dark brown eyes, she repeated, "Specifics."

"Yeah." He shrugged. "Wedding date. Place. Time. Guests."

"Oh, my," she muttered, and shook her head. "Suddenly this is getting so involved. So complicated."

"Would you prefer a whirlwind trip to Vegas?"

"Do I detect a hint of surliness in your tone?" she countered.

He frowned, walked to his desk and leaned one hip against the edge. "Not surly. Confused."

"Join the club," she muttered. For pity's sake, she'd hardly gotten used to the idea of being pregnant. Not to mention his spur-of-the-moment proposal. Now she was supposed to pull out a pad of paper and eagerly make out a guest list?

Come on. Even Wonder Woman would have needed a few days.

He folded his arms across his chest, cocked his head to one side and looked at her as though she was a particularly intriguing germ on a glass slide under a microscope. "I don't get it."

"What?" Stupid question.

"This about-face," he said. "A minute ago, we agreed that a marriage was the only answer. You *did* say yes, didn't you?"

She reached up and tucked her hair behind her ears. "Of course I said yes…"

"Then what's the problem?" he asked.

"How much time do you have?"

He smiled, God help her, and that lone dimple in his right cheek made its first appearance. Damn it. Why was she such a sucker for that dimple?

"All the time you need, Kate. Talk."

Talk. Easy enough for him to say. Hands locked tight behind her back, she paced again, feeling the need to burn off the excess energy that had her stomach roiling and her mind spinning. Back and forth, up and down, she looked at his office, the plain beige paint, the picture of the president, the dried-up splotches of the last rain on the windows and the half-dead ficus tree in the corner.

Talk. Where should she start? With ridiculous dreams or the painful reality?

She'd been hoping for so much more when she had put in a request for a transfer to Camp Pendleton.

For three years, Kate had loved Thomas Candello. And for those same three years, she'd kept quiet about it. She knew all too well his thoughts on marriage and love and happily-ever-after. He'd made no secret of the fact that his first marriage had been a disaster from the word *go* and that he had no intention of ever committing that particular mistake again.

So, wary of scaring him off, she'd patiently swallowed the three little words every time they threatened to roll off her tongue. She'd pretended to be as satisfied with their once-a-year tryst as he was. And she'd hoped that one day he would look into her eyes and see the love shining there and want to claim it.

So much for "hope springs eternal."

"Kate?" he prompted from his place by the desk. "What's going on?"

"Too much," she said and came to a stop by his office door. Turning around, she braced her back against it and looked at him from across the room. Unfortunately, distance didn't help. The liquid warmth in his eyes, that blasted dimple, his mouth, even several feet of empty space couldn't dilute their power. "Thomas," she said at last, "we can't just up and get married."

"Why not?" He pushed off the desk and started for her.

She held up one hand, stopping him in his tracks.

If he expected her to think, then he needed to give her some breathing room.

"We're both single adults. Unattached."

"Exactly."

He laughed shortly and shook his head. "Sorry, you lost me."

She sighed heavily. "In the month I've been here, we've hardly spoken more than once or twice."

"So?"

"So, don't you think people will be just a little bit curious if we announce our imminent wedding?"

"And if we don't get married, in a couple of months," he snapped a look at her still flat abdomen, "they'll be curious about a whole lot more than that."

"I know." She buried the flash of nerves that leaped into life in the pit of her stomach. "But still, we can't go from supposed strangers to newlyweds overnight."

He thought about it for a minute or two, then shrugged again. "Does it really matter? Is it anyone's business?"

"Yes," she said. "And no."

"Huh?"

"Yes, it does matter and no, it's not their business. But that won't stop the gossip and you know it."

"Military bases run on gossip. There's no way to avoid it."

"Maybe not, but we could slow it down a little."

He smiled. "What have you got in mind?"

"Dating?" she suggested.

This time he laughed. "Kate, we're a little beyond the dating stage, don't you think?"

"Okay, sure." She nodded and started pacing again, the sound of her heels against the linoleum tapping out a rhythm for her thoughts. "I suppose we could tell people that we've been seeing each other for three years."

"A *lot* of each other," he added.

"Yes, well, they don't need to know that, now do they?"

"Kate," Tom said, and crossed the room to her before she could stop him. "You're making this more difficult—more complicated than it has to be."

"I don't see how."

"We'll date," he said, and smiled down at her when she winced. "And after a whirlwind courtship, we'll have a nice, quiet wedding a few weeks from now."

"People will still talk."

"It won't matter. We'll be married. The talk will die down."

"Until I start showing."

"You can't prevent people from counting."

"I suppose," she said, and wished he would hold her again.

Tom reached for her, holding her tightly to him. He'd never seen Kate like this. Distracted. Worried— no, *scared.*

He pulled in a deep breath, enjoying the familiar, floral scent of her shampoo even as his mind told him she had a right to be scared, and if he had half a brain, he would be, too.

He'd done this before. He'd been married and

made a damn mess of it. He'd had a child, too, and blown that, as well.

Oh, yeah, he was just the guy Kate needed—an already-proven failure as a husband and father.

His stomach turned over, and a fist tightened inside it.

There were two ways this could go, he told himself. One, it could all blow up in his face, hurting him, Kate and the poor unsuspecting baby stuck with him as a father—or, it could be his chance to make up for doing everything so badly the first time around.

Heaven or hell.

The lady or the tiger.

Tom closed his eyes and held her more tightly.

A pounding headache throbbing behind her eyes, Kate sat at her desk, taking deep breaths and telling herself the worst was over. She'd told him about the baby. Nobody had fainted. He hadn't held up a rope of garlic to keep her at bay. And most important, she'd managed to keep her stomach from rebelling in the disgusting manner that was becoming all too familiar these days.

So why didn't she feel better?

Because it wasn't over. It was just beginning.

She was going to be a mother, God help the poor little thing nestled unknowingly inside her. And a wife. To a man who didn't want a wife.

Kate groaned out loud, pushed both hands through her short hair and held on to her skull to keep it from exploding. Trying to distract herself, she glared at the mountain of paperwork awaiting her attention. Files and folders and stapled sheafs of papers lay across her desk in what to anyone else's eye would look like a disorganized jumble. To Kate's credit, she knew what every single piece of paper was, where it belonged and how to put her finger on whatever was needed at a moment's notice.

That didn't mean she liked it.

Thomas was wrong, she thought, stealing a quick glance at the In pile that had grown substantially in the fifteen minutes she'd been gone. The military didn't run on gossip. It ran on paper. Piles and piles of paper.

A knock at the door delivered her and she looked up. "Yes?"

The door opened and her assistant, Staff Sergeant Eileen Dennis, poked her head in. "Excuse me, ma'am, but the other files have arrived."

"Perfect," Kate groaned and leaned back in her chair.

"Can I help, ma'am?" Eileen offered, stepping farther into the room and dropping at least ten more manilla folders onto an already precariously tilted stack.

Kate sighed. Tempting, but no. She might be pregnant and about to marry a reluctant groom, but she was still a Marine. And she could do her job—at least until her belly was so swollen she couldn't pull her chair in close enough to reach the desk.

She managed to stifle the groan building inside her as she scooted her chair in extra tight, just because she could.

Looking up at the younger woman standing opposite her, Kate figured Eileen Dennis to be about twenty-eight. Her bright blue eyes were sharp. Her smart cap of night black hair was regulation, yet somehow managed to look feminine. Spit and polish, the creases on the woman's uniform had creases. The staff sergeant was young, eager, dedicated and ambitious.

Everything Kate had always been herself. So why then did she suddenly feel like Grandma Moses in comparison?

"Thanks, Eileen," she said with a shake of her head. "I can manage."

She actually looked disappointed. "If you're sure…"

"I am," Kate said. "But if you can find me a cup of coffee, I'll put you up for promotion."

Eileen grinned at the joke. "Black, one sugar?"

"Yeah." Just as the door started to close, though, Kate said, "No. Wait." Caffeine. Not a good thing for growing babies. She caught Eileen's eye. "Make that tea."

"Tea, ma'am?" Surprise etched itself onto her features.

"Herbal." Lord, just saying it made her want to retch. How would she ever get through the next six months without a jolt of caffeine every day?

"Yes ma'am," Eileen said, and slowly closed the door again.

When she was alone, Kate pushed away from the desk and crossed the room to the one tiny window her office provided. Staring out at the busy base, she absently watched her fellow Marines carrying out their everyday tasks. The world was rolling right along, she thought. It didn't seem to matter that her own personal world lay in shambles at her feet.

Her phone rang and grudgingly Kate turned toward the desk again. She snatched it up on the third ring. "Yes?"

"Colonel Candello on line one, ma'am."

Her stomach twisted. Had he changed his mind already? Had the idea of a baby and marriage made him want to resign and catch the first sailboat to Tahiti?

A click, a hum, then Thomas's voice. "Kate?"

"I'm here."

A long pause. "You never agreed to dinner tonight. Let's get this courtship started."

So much for Tahiti.

"Tonight?" Her fingers tightened around the receiver.

"Any reason not to?"

She stared down at her desk, told herself she should work late and clear up all the files. But they'd be right there in the morning, waiting for her. "No," she said. "I guess not."

"Good. Seven?" he asked, and even over the phone his voice raised goosebumps on her skin. "I'll pick you up at your place?"

She rubbed one hand over her forearm, as if she could wipe away the effect he had on her.

"You don't know where I live," she said. Good heavens, she was marrying a man who didn't even know where her apartment was. This couldn't be right, could it? Right for any of them?

"I was hoping you'd tell me."

Kate sat down in her chair, propped her elbows on her desk and didn't even glance at the two manilla folders that slid off, spilling papers across her floor. "Thomas—" She rested her forehead in one palm. "This is all so weird. It feels…awkward."

"I know, honey," he said, his voice deepening into a low rumble of sound. "But we'll figure it all out."

She hoped so, because at the moment, her world felt about as steady as a ball twirling on the tip of a trained seal's snout.

"You still like Italian?" he asked.

Kate smiled, ridiculously pleased that he'd repeated the stupid little joke they traditionally used to start off their yearly week together. Even more ridiculous, his saying it now actually made her feel better. So she gave him the answer he was waiting for.

"I still like one Italian."

"That's a relief. You had me worried there for a minute, Kate." His chuckle carried across the line before he said, "So, Major. Give me your address so I can start sweeping you off your feet."

A moment later, Tom hung up. His hand still lying atop the cradled receiver, he stared blankly at the window opposite his desk. Weak winter sunshine fell through the spotty glass pane, painting a polka-dotted slash of gold across the linoleum.

All things considered, he told himself, that had gone pretty well. He flashed a look at the phone and frowned to himself. He'd managed to sound encouraging, uplifting and supportive without once letting his voice betray the sliver of panic that had torn his guts open at her news.

While he was on a roll, he snatched up the phone again and dialed his daughter's number. After two rings, she answered.

"Hi, kiddo," he said quickly.

"Hi, Dad, what's up?"

Way too much to go into over the phone, he thought. His fingers toyed with the curly telephone cord. "A change in plans. I can't make dinner tonight."

"Your loss," his daughter informed him. "I'm making Grandma's lasagna."

He smiled at the receiver. "Rain check?"

"Naturally," she said. "Anything wrong? You sound funny."

Funny? No, he didn't. He sounded exactly what he was. Terrified. But he wasn't going to say anything to Donna and her husband, First Sergeant Jack Harris, until he and Kate had had time to talk this whole thing out.

"No," he assured her. "Nothing's wrong." Then, because his whirlwind courtship was about to start, and she might as well start getting used to the idea, he said as casually as possible. "Actually, I have a date."

"Intriguing," his too-sharp daughter said. "Bachelor Colonel with a date. I haven't even seen you look at a woman since your barbecue a few months ago."

Just before his last trip to Japan, Tom remembered. He'd actually toyed with the idea of dating a woman he saw more than once a year. But, after dinner and a movie, he'd discovered that as nice as the woman was, she wasn't Kate.

"Who is she?" Donna prompted. "Anyone I know?"

"Major Katherine Jennings," he answered, and added silently, *Kate. The woman I've been having an affair with for three years. The mother of your new little brother or sister.* Oh, man.

"Nope," Donna told him. "Don't know her."

You will, he thought, but said only, "I've gotta go, kiddo."

"Okay, but you owe me," she warned. "Dinner here, next week?"

"Deal." Already moving to hang up, he said, "Say hello to Jack."

"Okay. 'Bye, Dad."

He set the phone down, Donna's last word ringing in his ears. Dad. Lord, he'd been a lousy parent the first time around. He swallowed back the knot of bitterness that always threatened to choke him when he recalled those lost years with Donna.

As teenagers he and Donna's mother had married with the best of intentions, only to see their relationship die within a couple of years. After the divorce, he'd concentrated solely on his career, moving up in the ranks—and he'd missed so much of Donna's childhood, he'd hardly known her when she had come to live with him when she was thirteen.

Shame simmered inside him, pushing him to his feet and demanding he move. He paced, unconsciously following the same path Kate's heels had trod only a few minutes ago.

Pregnant.

It had taken years to rebuild a relationship with Donna. Years filled with anxiety, frustration and the fear that he would never be able to overcome the "parenting" lessons he'd absorbed from his own father.

And now it would all start again. A knot of tension tightened in his gut. Was it fair to saddle some poor innocent baby with *him* as a father?

Just like the last time he'd gotten married, the bride would be carrying his child. God. Hadn't he learned *anything* in his forty-five years?

He rubbed both hands across his face viciously. A grown man, and he'd been as irresponsible as he had been at seventeen. A sad thing to note about yourself, he thought.

But instantly that night in Japan rolled back into his mind.

The two of them, locked together on that tiny balcony. Kate's flesh beneath his hands, her legs locked around his middle, the hot, tight feel of her body embracing his. In memory, he saw her head fall back, her lips form his name as another climax tore through her. He should have stopped then. Should have pulled away long enough to make sure she was safe. But he didn't. His greed for her had spilled through him, and he could no more have left her—even for a moment— than he could have stopped breathing on command.

So instead, with the sounds of the city far below them and the soft glow of the moon and a trillion stars above them, they'd created a life.

A life that had a right to expect a few little things like security and love from its parents.

Three

Tom pulled up in front of the small duplex, parked beneath the lamppost, set the brake and turned off the ignition. Opening the door, he pocketed the keys and slid out of his new truck.

Idly he ran one hand over the flashy red paint that looked a dingy gray in the weird glow of the yellow fog light. The day he'd bought it, just a month ago, he'd actually called Donna, to tease her about the "new baby" in his life.

A short laugh shot from his throat. *New baby* had suddenly taken on a completely different meaning.

He could just imagine the look on Donna's and her husband's faces when he announced the arrival of her little brother. Or sister.

Shaking his head, he started around the front of the car. A muffled roar of sound rolled toward him. Out of the darkness, four young boys appeared as shadows in the gloom, then sailed past him, ably surfing the asphalt on skateboards.

Their laughter hung in the air for a long minute after they were gone, and Tom stared after them. Skateboarding. In the dark. Fearlessly pitting themselves against drivers who would have a hard time spotting them in their blue jeans and sweatshirts.

A cold chill swept over him. The kids couldn't have been more than ten, tops. When his child was ten, Tom would be fifty-five. Nearly sixty. He groaned tightly. How in the hell would he be able to keep up with the kid?

Shaking his head at the thought, he turned to stare at the small, neat apartments in front of him. A single-story, craftsman-style duplex, Kate had told him hers was the one on the right. Tom shifted his gaze to the square of lamplight making the blue drapes across a wide front window glow with a nearly serene light. He tried to imagine her there, inside.

He should have come by sooner. Called her. He'd wanted to. But she was right. This did feel awkward. Sure, they'd known each other for three years. But they'd only spent three weeks of that time together.

In the month she'd been on base, Tom had hardly seen her. He'd deliberately kept his distance, wanting to give her time to settle in. To get used to the idea of their being in such close quarters for the first time.

But it had taken every ounce of his self-control to keep from calling her, talking to her. Honestly, he'd wanted to give her time to decide if she even wanted to continue the affair that had come to mean so much to him over the past three years.

Now, it seemed the choice had been made for her.

Dragging in a deep breath of sea-flavored air, he started for the front door. Along the way, he noted the neat flower border that lined the narrow, curved walk. Tiny statues of squirrels, chipmunks and rabbits dotted one half of the thumbnail-sized front lawn, and he smiled, wondering if Kate had set them out or if they belonged to her neighbor.

How little he knew about *her,* the person, he mused. Oh, he knew that rubbing the back of her knee lightly would make her purr in pleasure. But he didn't know the simple things. For instance, what was her favorite color?

What the hell kind of relationship was this?

Two front doors met him. The door on the left, painted a bright blue, also sported a wild-looking wreath made of dried flowers and boasting a stuffed canary on its straw ribbon. He glanced at it and it opened.

A small, older woman in skintight pink pants topped by a neon yellow sweatshirt stepped out onto her porch. She looked up at him, smiled and instantly lifted one hand to unnecessarily smooth her chic, silver hair. "Well," she said, her tone openly interested. "Hello. I heard you walk up, thought you were one of the girls. But you're most definitely not, so just exactly who are you?"

"Tom Candello, ma'am," he said, and couldn't help noticing when she winced slightly at the "ma'am."

She recovered quickly though and, stepping toward him, she held out her right hand. "Evie Bozeman," she said, giving him a wide smile. "You're here to see Kate, then?"

"That's right," he said, and snapped a quick look at the still-closed door on the right.

"And are you a Marine, too?" she practically cooed at him.

"Yes ma'am, I'm a colonel."

"Ooh, fascinating," she murmured, then her gaze swept him up and down. "A shame you didn't wear your uniform. I do so love a man in uniform."

"I don't usually wear it off base," he told her and silently counted his lucky stars that he hadn't worn it tonight, especially.

"As I said, a shame. Ah, well, jeans are nice, too." She inhaled sharply, beamed a smile at him and tightened her grip on his hand. "I'm delighted Kate has a date. I've told her and told her, she's too young to just sit at home all the time."

Too young, Tom thought with an inward groan. At thirty-two, she was too young for lots of things. Including him. As he'd told her often over the past three years.

"You take me, for example." Evie was talking again, tugging him toward Kate's door. "Why, I'm almost never home. Tonight's different, of course. The girls are coming over for a game of cards. We invited Kate to join us, but she said she had plans." She actually batted her eyelashes at him. "And she certainly wasn't lying."

There was a gleam in Evie Bozeman's eyes that had Tom wanting to call out the troops for backup.

From out on the street, a car horn sounded and Evie looked past him, thank heaven, squinted a bit, then grinned and waved. "The girls are here," she told him, and tugged him around again to face the walkway.

Tom glanced over his shoulder at Kate's unadorned door and wondered where the hell she was. Then it occurred to him that she might be watching all of this and thoroughly enjoying it instead of coming out to rescue him. As soon as that thought registered, though, he reminded himself that he was a colonel in the Marine Corps. He shouldn't have to be rescued from a woman who had to be at least sixty-five.

Determinedly he tried to pull his hand free, but Evie held on in a grip that told him she'd done this before.

"Now, don't run off, Tom," she said, waving one arm in a wide arc, to hurry her friends along the flower-lined walk. "I want you to meet the girls."

Surrendering to the inevitable, he followed her gaze to the four women hurtling up the walkway. Each one well into her sixties, they wore jeans or the same kind of tights Evie was wearing. Sweatshirts, T-shirts and running shoes completed the ensembles, and Tom had to admit they looked nothing at all like what he would expect from a bridge club.

"Girls," Evie announced proudly, "this is Tom." She paused for effect, then added, "He's a Marine. A *colonel*."

Tom shifted uneasily as four pairs of interested eyes turned on him.

"Where'd you find him, Evie?"

"My, what a looker!"

"Whose is he?"

"Can we keep him?"

This last from a tiny woman with carrot red hair and an eager glint in her eye.

Tom met that look and took an instinctive step backward. Where were all of the nice grandmotherly type women he'd known when he was a kid?

From behind him a door opened and he almost groaned in relief when he heard Kate say, "Tom?"

Taking advantage of Evie's surprise, Tom pulled his hand free and made a quick move for the blond woman standing in the open doorway. He didn't remember ever being so glad to see her as he was at this minute. The porch light glimmered on the lightest blond streaks in her hair, making the short, curled-under cut shimmer like silver and gold threads. The dress she wore was enough to destroy a lesser man, and the light, flowery scent he always associated with her enveloped him.

She smiled up at him as she closed and locked her front door behind her and his heart hammered against his chest. Yep, he told himself. Worse than a teenager.

An audible sigh of disappointment came from "the girls."

"Hello, Kate," Evie said brightly. "I was just introducing Tom to my friends."

"So I see," she said, and fought down a ripple of excitement that shook through her when Tom's arm brushed against her. She didn't even want to think about the look she'd seen in his eyes a moment ago.

"Going someplace nice, are you?" Evie asked, her gaze fastening on Kate's dark blue, brushed-wool dress.

"I don't know," Kate said, shooting a look at Tom. "Are we?"

He rubbed one hand across the back of his neck. "I was thinking about the Pasta Pot."

"Good choice," Evie told him, then began to herd her friends toward her front door. "Have a nice night. And Kate? Maybe you can join us for cards next week?"

"I'd like that," Kate said, smiling at the woman who'd become a friend in the past month.

"I didn't know you played bridge," Tom muttered.

Before she could correct him, her neighbor did it for her.

"Bridge!" Evie exclaimed on a laugh. "That's for old women. We play poker, honey, down and dirty."

"Poker?" Tom repeated, and Kate dipped her head to hide a smile.

"Five-card stud. Wimps and wusses need not apply." She sailed into her apartment with a wave and a high-pitched "Toodle-oo!"

After a long moment of stunned silence, Tom muttered, "Now there goes a completely terrifying woman."

The tension she'd felt all afternoon shattered, Kate looked up at him and laughed. "Wonderful, isn't she?"

"Interesting," he said, then confessed, "For a minute there, when 'the girls' arrived, I knew just what it felt like to be a nicely browned Thanksgiving turkey when dozens of hungry eyes are locked on it.''

Kate looked him up and down quickly, covertly and couldn't really blame Evie and the others. He looked good enough to eat. Black hair with just a dusting of gray at the temples. A red knit shirt that stretched tight across his muscled chest and broad shoulders was tucked into the narrow waistband of a pair of jeans that hugged his long, truly great legs. No wonder Evie and her friends had briefly captured him. It wasn't every day a gorgeous man wandered up that walk.

Something inside her quivered, like a guitar string plucked and left to vibrate. Kate swallowed hard and strived for a calm, easy tone in her voice as she said, ''When I first moved in, Evie made me dinner every night for a week. Said I shouldn't have to bother with anything other than unpacking because moving was such a bitch.''

He chuckled, and the sound brought back memories of black nights, starlit skies and soft music. She could almost feel his warm breath on her neck. Almost taste the champagne they'd used to toast each other their last night together. The night they'd made a baby.

A shriek of laughter rose up from next door, and Tom glanced that way, unaware of Kate's spiraling thoughts. ''She's something, all right,'' he said. ''I look at her and try to imagine my own mother wearing that outfit.''

''And can't?'' she asked, dropping her keys into her purse and starting down the walk.

"Angelina Candello?" he asked as he followed her. "In *neon?* I don't think so."

"Angelina's a beautiful name," she said softly and waited for him to unlock the truck door.

"Yeah." He held it open for her. "You would have liked her."

"Would have?"

"She died about six years ago."

"I'm sorry."

He shrugged but she caught a glint of remembered pain shining briefly in his eyes. Then he closed the door and walked around the hood to climb in beside her. As he fired the engine and pulled away from the curb, Kate watched him, her mind racing.

Three years, she thought. Three years she'd known him and yet she really knew so little. Swallowing back the sadness welling inside her, she asked quietly, "Your father?"

"Died when I was a kid." Tom kept his eyes on the road, "Angie raised me. What about you?"

Kate's hands smoothed the fall of her dress across her knees and watched the ripple of material as she said, "I never knew my father. My mother died when I was fifteen."

"So we're both orphans."

She shot a look at him from beneath lowered lashes. "Yes. I guess we are."

Another long moment of silence stretched out between them until finally, when they stopped at a red light, Tom spoke. Gently he asked, "Do you realize how little we know about each other?"

"Strange, isn't it?" Strange and sad and lonely.

She'd loved him from the moment she laid eyes on him. She could map every inch of his body from memory. She'd held him inside her, found magic in his touch and was now sheltering his child within her and she didn't even know his middle name.

"What *is* your middle name?" she asked abruptly, determined to start mining him for information.

He stared at her, brow furrowed in confusion. "My middle name?"

"It's a place to start, don't you think?" She crossed her legs, black silk stockings swishing. She linked her shaking hands around her knee.

Someone behind them honked, and Tom turned his head forward and stepped on the gas.

"Yeah, all right." He nodded and moved into the left lane. The fingers of his left hand tapped nervously against the steering wheel. "Nice night."

She stared at him as he steered the truck into a well-lit parking lot. When he didn't say anything else, she commented, "You're stalling."

"Hmm? Why would I be stalling?"

"You don't want to tell me your middle name."

"That's ridiculous." He snorted a laugh as he pulled into a parking slot, set the brake and killed the engine.

"I think so."

He winced. "You haven't heard it yet."

A smile tugged at the corners of her mouth. Was he embarrassed? Another piece of information to add to the paltry store of things she knew about the man she loved.

Kate locked her fingers together tighter to keep

from reaching out to touch him. In the dim, muted glow of the overhead lights, his face was shadowed but she still read the stubborn reluctance on his features.

"Okay," she said softly, "now I *have* to hear it."

One corner of his mouth tilted up, and that dimple of his creased his cheek. Kate's stomach flipped and she forced air into her lungs in an effort to quiet it.

"This is top secret, Major," he warned, giving her a mock glare.

"Sir!" she snapped, and freed one hand long enough to give him a sharp salute.

"I'm serious," he said. "Only a handful of people know what I'm about to tell you.

"I'm honored."

"I'm embarrassed."

"I noticed."

"Fine." Frowning, he leaned in close and muttered, "Salvatore."

Kate pulled back and looked at him. "You're kidding."

"Would I make that up?"

No, she supposed not. Aloud, she tried it out. "Thomas Salvatore Candello. Hmm."

"It gets worse."

Her eyes widened. "There's more?"

"Thomas Salvatore Giovanni Candello."

"Wow."

He nodded sagely. "Now you understand the reason for secrecy."

Actually her hormones were making her just sappy enough to find his full name sort of...romantic. But instead of saying so, she told him, "Your secret's safe, Colonel."

"It had better be, Major," he said with another warning look. "Now it's my turn. Give."

"Give?"

"The middle name, Major. Let's have it." He crooked one finger at her.

"It's not nearly as...interesting as yours."

"Undoubtedly," he admitted. "Still. Fair's fair."

"It's Marie," she said. "Katherine Marie."

He looked at her for the space of several heartbeats, then smiled softly. "It's beautiful."

Something inside her trembled.

"*You're* beautiful," he added, and leaned toward her again. "Lord, I've missed you, Kate."

"Thomas...," she said on a sigh and wasn't sure if she'd meant it as an invitation or a warning. His eyes flashed and in their depths she read his hunger. His desire. She recognized it effortlessly because she was sure the same emotions were glittering in her own eyes. It happened every time he got within three feet of her.

But this wasn't supposed to happen tonight. Their first real chance to talk since she'd arrived in California, heaven knew they had plenty to talk *about*. All afternoon she'd reminded herself that this was a night for conversation—not for picking up where they left off in Japan.

Steeling herself with that thought, she unsnapped her seat belt, opened the truck door and swiveled to climb out.

"Kate?"

She turned to look at him. With a helpless shrug she said, "If you start kissing me now, Thomas, we'll never get anything settled."

He pulled in a deep breath, held it, then exhaled in a rush. Nodding briskly, he muttered, "You're right. First things first."

When they met at the back of the truck and he took her arm to escort her into the restaurant, though, he paused, waiting until she looked up at him. "But you have to know how much I want you, Kate."

She shivered beneath his touch and the fiery sparks in his eyes. "Believe me, Thomas," she assured him. "I know."

The Pasta Pot was small, and the crowd friendly. A veritable jungle of flowers and ivy spilled out of baskets hanging from the wide oak beams overhead. Candles dotted every table and the flickering flames looked like fireflies in the atmospheric gloom.

On a weeknight, there was no wait for a table, and Tom walked behind Kate and the hostess to a corner booth in the back. Once their orders had been taken by a waitress who attended them promptly, Tom turned his full attention on Kate.

"It's pretty," she said, glancing around the room as the muted strains of Beethoven floated to them from the overhead speakers.

"Food's good, too," he said.

Her gaze slid to his. "This is so weird."

"Yeah," he agreed and reached across the gleaming oak table to lay one hand over hers. "But we'll work it out."

At that, something inside her seemed to burst. She

started talking, and the words poured from her like water from an upended bucket.

"I can't believe this is happening," she started with a shake of her head. "How can we do this? How can we get married? We hardly know each other."

"We knew each other well enough to make a baby," he pointed out.

"A baby." She propped her elbows on the table and cradled her head in her hands. "Ohmigod. How can I be a mother?" she muttered, more to herself than to him. "I can't cook, I don't sew," she threw him a wild look. "I can't even bake cookies, for Pete's sake! Shouldn't a mother know how to bake cookies? Isn't that a requirement?"

"I don't think so," he said and tried to smile. "As far as I know, you don't have to be able to chop wood, stoke a fire or slaughter your own meat anymore, either."

She groaned and shook her head. "You don't understand, Thomas. I don't even keep plants. They always die. No matter what I do," she went on, now tangling her fingers together and squeezing. "Too little water, too much water, no fertilizer, too much fertilizer, sunlight, shade...doesn't matter. I kill 'em all."

"Kate..." He smiled. "It's not the same thing."

"An indiscriminate plant killer, Thomas." She met his gaze, and he saw with heartstopping clarity the sheen of tears beginning to well in her eyes. "I've been blacklisted in every garden nursery from here to Guam. So I ask you," she added as she blinked those tears back, "is this the kind of person who should be a mother?"

He slid closer to her on the maroon leather booth seat and pulled her into his arms for a quick hug. Something inside him tightened painfully, then relaxed again with an almost painful release. "You'll be great," he said confidently.

"How can you know that?"

"Because you care so damn much," he whispered. "That's all the baby will need. Heck, that's all the three of us will need to make this work, Kate. Caring." He ran one finger along her cheek gently. "If we care enough, everything else will take care of itself." Tom repeated that last phrase to himself silently and hoped to God he was right. "Trust me, Kate."

Four

Every night for three nights running, he took her out, determined, as he said, to get this whirlwind courtship up and running. Dinner the first night, a movie the second and a play at the Performing Arts Center the third. And after every date, he gave her a kiss at her front door and left.

At first, she'd thought it sweet. As if they really were just beginning to date. But lately, she'd begun to wonder if he simply didn't want her anymore.

Maybe taking a pregnant woman to bed didn't rank high on his list of priorities. And then again, maybe he was already resenting her. Resenting the baby and this marriage and trying to find a discreet way out of it.

Kate wrapped her arms around her tightly and threw a glance at the old, walnut mantel clock perched on a low bookcase near the drape-covered front window. In ten minutes he would be pulling up out front to take her to the Starlight Room in Seal Beach for dancing.

Dancing.

She glanced down at the black dress and three-inch heels she wore. All dressed up and now she didn't want to go anywhere. What she wanted was a chance to find out if Thomas still felt anything for her or if he was simply picking up a burden he accepted as his responsibility.

Damn it, she needed to know. She loved him. Always had. But how would he ever come to love her if he already resented her? And what kind of life would their child have, growing up in a house cold with dislike?

No. If that was their future, she had to know it now. When there was still time to change it. Single motherhood could cost her her career, and heaven knew the very idea of raising a child on her own terrified her—but those options were preferable to life with a man who couldn't stand the thought of touching her.

From outside came the deep rumble of his truck's engine. Kate's heartbeat staggered as she walked to the door. Her full black skirt swished around her knees, her heels tapped lightly against the polished wood floor. A swirl of nerves rose up in the pit of her stomach, but she reminded herself that this was the man she loved. The man whose touch could melt her bones. This time her stomach did a series of flip-flops, and she took several breaths to settle it. Now was not the time for her sporadic morning-afternoon-night sickness to kick in.

She opened the door and watched as he hurried up the walk. His dark brown jacket, tan pants, white shirt and dark green tie suited him every bit as well as jeans and T-shirts or his uniform. No doubt about it, he was a gorgeous man, and just looking at him sent ripples of anticipation running along her spine.

It was time to discover if he still felt the same.

As he approached, he shot a wary glance toward Evie's door. Since that first night, Evie had waylaid him twice more and each time had been more reluctant to let him go than the time before.

He sprinted the last few steps and slipped inside. Only when the door was safely closed behind him did he take a moment to look at her. A slow smile crossed his face and he whistled, low and long.

"Major, you look fantastic."

"Thanks," she said and led the way to the living room.

"Are you set to go?" he asked. "Our dinner reservations are for seven-thirty."

"Would you mind if we didn't go out?" She sat down on the sofa and waited while he crossed the room to take a seat beside her. Not too close. Not too far away.

"Are you feeling all right?"

"I'm fine," she said. "I just don't feel like dancing, I guess."

"Okay," Tom leaned back into the cushions and folded his arms across his chest to keep from reaching for her. That black dress of hers should be against the law, he thought, as a tight fist of desire slugged him in the stomach. The low-cut, vee neckline was enough to destroy a man, dragging his gaze to the swell of her breasts and then denying him a peek.

She leaned toward him slightly, and his eyes narrowed. The tops of her breasts pillowed against the black, slinky fabric and the contrasts of pale and dark shook him to the bone. He'd been trying to give her what she wanted. A chance for them to come to know each other. The time to ease into what would be their new relationship. But if something didn't snap soon, he would.

There was just so much a man could take.

"Thomas," she said, her voice a whispered hush, intimate, sexy. "I'd rather just stay in tonight, if you don't mind."

Mind? He'd like nothing better than to have her to himself for a few hours. Preferably naked, of course.

He didn't say so, though. "Sure. Whatever you want."

Still she leaned toward him, and he felt his control weakening even as one part of his body became granite hard. Her light, floral scent drifted to him, tearing at his insides, filling his mind with erotic memories of nights spent in this woman's arms.

He wanted her more than his next breath, and there was no use denying it any longer. She was pregnant with his child, they would be married soon and none of that mattered. All that counted now was the shimmer in her eyes and the emptiness of his arms.

He leaned in toward her.

Kate held her breath as he drew closer. Her heart

fluttered wildly in her chest, her lungs strained for the air she was suddenly too weak to give them, and her mouth went completely dry.

It was still there. That passionate bond between them. She felt its strength.

Electricity dazzled the air as it had from the moment they'd met three years before. He reached for her, and when his hand cupped the back of her head, drawing her down toward him, she felt the sizzling imprint of each of his fingers. Close. So close. His breath brushed against her, soft and warm. She inhaled the sharp, tangy scent of his cologne and fell into the hot, liquid center of his eyes.

Then his mouth dusted across hers. Once. Twice. Gently at first as if retracing a route that was both familiar and new to him. Air staggered into her lungs. Her mind went deliciously blank just as her body kicked into startled life.

All she could think of was Thomas. The nearness of him. And the long, lonely months they'd been apart.

As if he sensed her feelings and shared them, he groaned deeply, snaked his free arm around her waist and dragged her across the small space separating them.

Tearing his mouth from hers, he buried his face in the crook of her neck, teeth nibbling, tongue adoring. And in between lavish kisses, he murmured, "You taste so good. Smell so incredible. I've missed you, Kate. More than you'll ever know. I've missed you."

"Oh, Thomas," she whispered, letting her head fall

back on her neck, inviting his kiss, his touch. "It's been too long."

"Three months, Kate,' he said on another groan and ran the tips of his fingers down the vee neckline of her dress. "Damn, but right now it feels like years."

She shivered and lifted herself up in his arms, arching her breasts toward him, hoping he would push the soft fabric aside and take her flesh into his hands. Kate reached for his tie and with trembling fingers undid the knot and popped free the first two buttons of his shirt. She slid one hand beneath the white cotton and trailed her palm across his skin, delighting in the warm, solid strength of him.

He tensed beneath her touch. She felt his muscles bunch as he shifted position on the couch and pulled her into his lap. Beneath her, his hard body tightened further, and she wiggled her hips, deliberately torturing them both.

Lifting his head, he caught her eye and gave her a slow, wicked grin. "Want to play, huh?" Then his right hand skimmed up the length of her silk-clad legs and under the hem of her dress.

She gasped and held her breath as his fingers danced along her inner thighs, coming to rest at the top of her garter-held stockings.

A throb of pure, feminine pleasure rocked her. She knew very well what stockings did to him. Had discovered that particular weakness of his their first week together, in Hawaii. Ruthlessly she'd exploited that weakness since, every chance she got. In a brief, detailed flash, the memory of that first time shot through her mind on Fast Forward.

Dressing for dinner while he showered, she'd just finished adjusting her black lace garter belt when he'd stepped from the bathroom ringed by a cloudy mist of hot steam.

He'd taken one look at her, dropped his towel and informed her they'd be calling for room service. Then, she recalled hazily, he'd spent the next half hour working those garters free with his teeth.

Even the memory had deep heat pooling in her center and she trembled in response.

"You're killing me here, Kate," he mumbled and dipped his head to taste the pulse point at the base of her throat. At the same time, his fingertips crept higher, sliding across black silk, then creamy, smooth flesh to find the warm heart of her, hidden beneath a wisp of lace.

As his hand cupped her and she squirmed in his grasp, he proved he, too, had a good memory by whispering, "Room service?"

She moaned tightly and caught his face between her palms. "We'll call for pizza later," she said, then kissed him with everything she had.

Who the hell needed pizza? he thought.

He had all he wanted right here in his arms.

She shifted slightly in his grasp, turning toward him, brushing her breasts against his chest, and he suddenly wanted to tear her dress away so that he could lose himself in the soft, creamy texture of her skin. He wanted—no, needed—to feel her again. To touch her, explore her body as if for the first time.

His right hand slid from the center of her heat to smooth across the lacy garters and the tops of her nylons. He knew she wore the things to drive him insane. And damn it, it worked every time.

In the months apart from her, she'd crowded his dreams. The memories of her long, stocking-clad legs tortured him. Visions of her soft blue eyes haunted him. Snatches of her laughter plagued his memory. And now she was here. And it was almost more than he could stand.

He had to have her. Had to watch passion and pleasure darken her eyes. Had to bury himself within her. Claim her as he'd done before. Feel the release and the sweet satisfaction he'd only found with her.

He wanted to hear his name sigh from her lips as her body convulsed around his.

His blood roaring in his ears, Tom bent his head to kiss her, plundering her mouth with his tongue, driving the air from her lungs and into his. She moaned, from deep in her throat, and the soft, strangled sound shattered what little control he had left.

Lifting his head again, he flipped the hem of her skirt back to her waist, exposing her trim, white thighs and the black silk covering them.

He looked his fill and fed the blood rushing to his groin. Rock hard and ready, he ran the flat of his hand across her thigh and up, toward the heat waiting for him.

"Thomas!" she whispered brokenly even as her hips arched slightly off his lap and into his hand.

"I need you, Kate," he muttered and his voice strained with the desire nearly choking him. "Now. I need you now."

"Now," she urged breathlessly.

His fingertips slipped beneath the flimsy strip of elastic lining the morsel of black lace that was her panties. In a heartbeat, with a flick of his wrist, he'd torn it aside.

Kate trembled, but he read the passion in her eyes and knew she was as hungry as he. Knew she felt the same fire building inside.

It had always been like this between them.

Heat. Steam. Overpowering need.

His fingertips brushed her core and she moaned. Again, he touched her, smoothing his fingers across the soft, tender flesh, adjusting his caresses according to the whimpers issuing from her throat.

Kate lifted herself into his hand, wanting him to touch her deeper, harder. More than anything, she needed to feel connected to him. She'd been so alone these past few months. Had felt even more so since learning about the baby. Her mind and heart had been torn. Her world left crumbling around her, and until now there'd been nothing to hold on to. No one.

Or so she'd thought.

But there had been Thomas. When she'd needed his support most, he'd given it to her without hesitation. He'd dated her and courted her. And now, he gave her the closeness she'd craved. And the knowledge that, yes, he did still want her. Did still feel the powerful, emotional bond that existed between them.

His fingers dipped into her warmth and she trembled at the gentle yet determined invasion. So right. So right. Her hips bucked as his touch electrified her body, sending every nerve into humming awareness.

Again and again, he touched her, his fingers, his thumb brushing across her most sensitive spot. His mouth took hers and she held his face between her palms. Parting his lips with her tongue, she imitated the movement of his fingers, darting in and out of his mouth until he was as breathless as she.

Fireworks exploded inside her. She felt the heat. Saw the colors flash from beneath her closed eyes. Greedy for him, as she'd always been, she held him tightly, her fists closing on his shirt at the shoulders.

They'd always had this, she told herself. No matter what else had occurred between them, this sexual magic existed. Real and powerful, it careened wildly around them like ball lightning captured inside a tiny room with nowhere to go.

When the first rippling sensation began to unwind within her, Kate tensed and planted her feet on the sofa cushions. Lifting her hips high off his lap, she strained to capture that always-elusive moment of complete and total satisfaction.

"Take it, Kate," he whispered, tearing his mouth from hers. "Let the feeling take you. Surrender."

She felt his gaze locked on her face and opened her eyes wide to meet his. Staring into the warm, chocolate gaze that watched her so tenderly, she gave herself over to the waves crashing through her, over her, around her. Her body trembled. Her head fell back. She called out his name as she crested the peak and slowly slid down the other side, safe in the circle of his arms.

"Ah, Kate," Tom murmured, his heart racing, his body aching. He buried his face in the crook of her neck, nibbling, tasting, teasing. Needing to touch her, to be a part of her.

She stirred and beneath his fingers began to twitch and writhe again. "Thomas," she said, and her voice was a pale hush of sound. "I need you inside me, Thomas. Now."

Her words fueled the hunger riding him. He needed that, too. More than he ever had before, he wanted to slide into her depths and feel her body surround him, hold him.

Teeth tightly clenched, he shifted to one side, laid her down on the couch and stood up to tear off his own clothes.

She struggled up into a sitting position and quickly tugged her dress up and off over her head. But when she reached to undo the tiny front clasp of her bra, he stopped her. "Don't," he nearly pleaded. "Let me."

A soft smile curved her mouth as she lay back down and parted her black silk clad thighs for him.

Tom's breath hitched in his chest and he wouldn't have been surprised if it had stopped altogether. Against the blue and green tapestry covered sofa, she looked magnificent. All light and shadow, pale flesh and black lace. She was any man's fantasy and his reality.

He tossed his clothes onto the floor and knelt over her. His thumb and forefinger flipped the clasp of her bra free and he eased the fragile fabric aside, cupping her breasts in the palms of his hand. Her nipples pebbled under his touch, their rosy tips hardening delicately.

She bit down hard on her bottom lip as he caressed her, arching her back, letting half moans slide from her throat. Her pulse beat throbbed at the base of her neck as she lifted her hands to draw his head down toward her.

Tom bent and took first one nipple and then the other into his mouth. Lips and tongue teased, working her flesh with tender deliberation. She gasped when he suckled her, then moaned in abandonment as he left one breast for the other.

Her passion fed his own. Her sighs reached inside him, twisting his heart and soul together, making them one. Making him complete. Filling the void that only she could touch.

He didn't question that. Didn't stop to think what it might mean. For now, for tonight, this was all that mattered.

And when he couldn't stand the wait another moment, he eased up, cupped her bottom in his hands and slid into the heat he'd known would be waiting for him. Surrounded by her, he groaned tightly and moved, slowly at first, as if to savor the sensation of once again finding her haven. Then as the need grew and blossomed inside him, he moved more quickly. Thrust after thrust, driving them both toward the end that was racing toward them.

Seconds became moments. Moments became eternities.

Further, deeper, higher. He couldn't think. Could only feel. A glorious, all-encompassing greed for her grabbed him, shook him and pushed him on. Only with her. Only with Kate had he ever found this white hot place where passion and need flowered together.

She met his movements fiercely, eagerly. Her hands clutched at his shoulders. Her nails dug into his skin, branding him. Her head tipped back into the cushions. Kate groaned his name, held on and welcomed it all, holding it to her as tightly as she did him.

Tom felt her muscles contract around him, and he groaned her name like a prayer as his body erupted, pouring everything he was into her depths.

Five

A slow tear seeped from the corner of her eye, rolled along her temple and disappeared into the tangled mess of her fine, blond hair.

Kate wasn't even sure why she was crying. What they'd just shared had been so perfect. So beautiful. Her body still hummed with satisfaction and she definitely had the answer to the question that had been plaguing her.

Thomas still wanted her. Despite the bizarre situation they found themselves in.

She inhaled a shaky breath and told herself that at least it was a place to start. If he felt passion and desire and want, then was it such a stretch to hope that one day he might feel love?

Whether he could admit it or not, there was already a powerful connection between them. She knew very well how he felt about love. He'd made no secret of his feelings over the past three years. He wasn't interested in it, he'd said countless times. He preferred what they had together. No strings. No complications.

Her heart twisted painfully.

He muttered something and shifted a bit.

Kate held him to her, unmindful of his weight pressing her down into the cushions. For the moment she simply wanted to enjoy the feel of his hard, warm body aligned with hers. Thinking could come later. Heck, *breathing* could come later.

"Kate?" His whisper came in a low rumble of sound, bristling along her still-sensitive nerve endings and jangling together in the pit of her stomach. "I'm going to squash you in another minute."

"I'm fine," she said just as quietly. Besides, if he moved now, he might see the telltale track of her tear before she had a chance to wipe it away. Blast it, she didn't want to start crying.

Yet tears seemed to be too close to the surface these days. Why did hormones have to be so involved with pregnancy, anyway?

Despite her grip on him, he levered himself up onto one elbow and stared down at her just as she moved to swipe her hand across the side of her face. Instantly his eyes narrowed on the trail of dampness that one tear had left behind.

"Crying?" he asked, clearly worried now. "I made you cry?"

"Thomas," she started to say.

He rolled to one side of her on the wide, comfortable sofa and looked at her steadily. "Did I hurt you?" A pause and then, "The baby?"

"No," she said, disgusted with herself and her blasted hormones. "Of course not."

"Then why?"

More tears suddenly swam in her eyes, blurring her vision. Angrily she brushed them away with the backs of her hands. "I don't know why," she muttered. "The other day, I actually cried over a phone company commercial."

He smiled, but she could see he was unconvinced.

"Thomas," she said, laying one hand on his chest, loving the feel of his heartbeat thudding against her fingertips. "You didn't hurt me," she said, willing him to believe her. "It's just...I'm..." She searched for the perfect word to describe what she was feeling and couldn't find it. At the moment she would have required an entire dictionary, complete with thesaurus. Flopping back down onto the cushion helplessly, she half wailed, "I don't even know what I am anymore."

"Pregnant?"

She flung one hand across her eyes so she wouldn't have to look at him. "Yes," she said on a tight groan. "I guess that about covers it. What the heck are we going to do about this?"

"I thought we had that settled," he said, lifting her hand away so that he could watch her eyes. "We're getting married."

Much to her own disgust, Kate's bottom lip trembled. Married. Over the past three years, she'd imagined him saying those words to her countless times.

Only in her dreams it was so different. So romantic. So "I can't live without you, marry me fast."

Never once had she imagined a good, old-fashioned shotgun wedding.

Logically she supposed she should be pleased that he was saying it at all, since it would make her career, her life and the baby's life so much easier to manage. But as she'd long since realized, logic and Thomas rarely met up in her thoughts.

Her mind raced on, spinning out visions of the next twenty years or so. Images spiraled in front of her. Married, she and Thomas stayed together for the sake of their child and the great sex. From here on out, they'd go through life hardly talking, yet wearing out one mattress after another. Their poor child would probably never see them since they would rarely leave the bedroom. The two of them would never get to know each other because that would involve actual speech occasionally. They would spend their entire lives as though it was one long, weekend affair.

And while some people might look on that as a good thing, Kate wanted more. She'd loved him for three years and had hoped to convince him that he loved her, too.

Oh, yeah, she thought, heart breaking into tiny, jagged-edged splinters, this was going to work out swell.

He was talking, she suddenly realized, and pushed her depressing thoughts aside to pay attention.

"I thought a simple wedding, at my house, would be good."

"Your house."

"Well, yes," he said. "It's a big place, built for

entertaining.'' He eased down beside her and pulled her close. "We could even hold the ceremony in the backyard, if you wanted to.''

"Thomas, what kind of marriage is this going to be?''

"What do you mean?''

"I mean," she said, and turned her head to look at him. "Are we really doing the right thing?''

Tom stared into her blue eyes and asked himself the same thing. As he had dozens of times over the past few days. "Who knows what the *right* thing is, Kate?'' he grumbled. Lord knew, he'd been trying to answer that one since the day she'd told him about the baby.

"Shouldn't we try to figure it out?''

"Should we?'' he asked. "Maybe there isn't an answer.'' He sat up on the couch, then turned his head to look at her. "Look, I'm not a good bet at marriage, I admit that. Hell, I've told you all about Donna's mother and what a mess I made of things.''

"That's not what I was talking about,'' she said, and sat up beside him.

"It's what I think about,'' he countered. "Ever since you told me about the baby, all I've thought about is what might go wrong this time.'' He shoved one hand through his hair. "Don't you see? I come from a *long* line of lousy fathers. From generation to generation, the men in my family have screwed up fatherhood. Hell, I didn't even get to know Donna until she was half-grown! This could be a second chance for me. To be involved with my kid's childhood. To somehow make right what I did wrong with Donna. Hopefully.''

He glanced at her and couldn't read her expression. Maybe that was for the best. ''On the other hand, I don't want to cheat you.''

'Cheat me?'' she repeated.

''Yeah.'' He reached out and smoothed her hair back from her face, then let his hand drop. ''I told you when we started this...''

''Affair?'' she offered.

''Fine. Affair. I told you then, I wasn't interested in love. Or commitment. Or anything else that I've already failed at so miserably.''

''I know that.''

''The thing is,'' he said as if she hadn't interrupted, ''should you have to go through your life not being loved as you should be loved?'' He shook his head and moved for the edge of the couch. ''Seems like you're getting the short end of this particular stick, Major. If you want to rethink this whole thing, I'd understand.''

She turned and scooted off the sofa. ''So you're saying you're willing to get married, you just don't want to. Is that it?''

Tom shot her a quick look and shook his head. Living his life out with a woman who lit up his insides like a bonfire wouldn't be unbearable. He just had to make it clear that as much as he wanted her, he wouldn't love her. Couldn't love her.

And no. He didn't want to be married. Had avoided it neatly for years. But the situation had changed.

Duty was something he recognized, respected. And his duty here was clear.

"I asked you to marry me, Kate. I'll do my best by you and the baby. But I can't promise more than that."

She nodded, and her hair fell forward, hiding her expression.

"And something else you have to remember." Might as well get this all out now as later. There were more than a couple of points they hadn't gotten around to discussing yet. Points that would have a major impact on their lives.

Her head snapped up and she looked at him.

"My tour at Pendleton is almost over. In another six months or so, I'll be transferred," he reminded her.

"I know that." She hugged herself tightly.

"And you just got here," Tom continued, even though he knew she was aware of the situation. "You know as well as I do that married officers don't always land the same assignment."

"I know the regulations as well as you do," Kate muttered darkly. "Married officers are guaranteed three years out of every nine together."

"It's not much," he said, and a surprising part of him regretted it.

"No, it's not." Her arms seemed to tighten around herself as if she was looking for stability.

He didn't blame her. Even though they would be married, a lot of the time, she might still be a single parent. Unless they took turns being primary parent.

God, this was just getting more jumbled the deeper they got into it.

"I want you to know, though," he said, "when we decided to get married, I requested bases around here for my new assignment."

She looked at him then, but her eyes were unreadable. He wished he could say something—anything—that would take the defensiveness out of her posture. But there was nothing.

"There's no guarantee I'll get one of the California bases, but I wanted you to know I'm trying."

She inhaled deeply and nodded. "None of this is going to be easy, Thomas. I know that. And I appreciate what you're doing. I really do."

"But?" he prompted, since he definitely heard an unspoken hesitation in her words.

Kate shook her head.

"At least we have this going for us," he said, and he gave her a half smile.

"This?" she whispered.

"Sex," he explained. "We share passion, and that's more than a lot of people have."

"Passion tends to flare up and burn out. Then what?"

"We've been 'flaring' now for three years," he reminded her. "No sign of burnout yet."

"One week, once a year," she muttered. "Heck, this isn't even a full-fledged affair. It's a yearly vacation with perks."

"And that's bad?" His smile quirked a bit higher.

"No," she said almost to herself, shaking her head and pushing off the couch. As she collected her clothes, she continued. "But marriage has to be more than passion, Thomas. It has to be based on more than sex or that's all we'll ever have."

He watched her. Couldn't help himself. As she bent over to pick up her dress and the bra he'd slipped off her shoulders, he admired the curve of her behind. And those garters and stockings were rekindling the fire he'd only just put out.

Why did she have to make this more complicated than it already was? They'd made a baby together, and together they'd raise it. And along the way, they could enjoy each other.

"I don't know what you're worried about, Kate," he said softly. "There's more than the sex between us. We get along. We like each other."

She straightened up, tossed her hair back out of her eyes and clutched her dress in front of her like some ancient talisman. "Now, *there's* a high recommendation."

He met her gaze squarely, evenly. Swallowing back a slight simmer of irritation, he reached down and grabbed up his shorts and slacks. "Kate, I care for you. More than I have any other woman I've ever known."

She stiffened and tightened her grip on that dress.

He stood up opposite her and dressed as he talked. "But I'm forty-five years old, Kate."

"This has nothing to do with—"

"Thirteen years older than you." He cut her off, continuing his little speech. "Old enough to know firsthand that love isn't a cure-all for everything, and most often, it just botches things up right before it explodes in your face."

Lifting her chin, she said tightly, "I'm not asking for undying pledges of love here, Thomas."

"Then what?" His chest felt tight, as though an unseen hand was squeezing his heart in a cold fist.

"If we're going to be married, then I think we owe it to ourselves and our child to make it the best marriage we can."

Reasonable. "Agreed."

"With mutual respect," she added.

"I go along with that."

"And no more sex."

"What?" He stared at her, hoping to see a flash of humor in her eyes. But it wasn't there. She meant what she was saying. "You can't be serious. A celibate marriage?"

She sniffed and pulled her dress on over her head. Wriggling into it, she shook her hair back from her face and stared at him. "At first, yes."

"At first?" He sounded like a damned parrot and didn't really care. He clung to those two words like a drowning man snatching at a piece of driftwood.

Kate inhaled slowly, deeply before speaking again in a calm, rational tone. "I just think it would be best if we didn't sleep together right away. If we took our time."

He cocked his head and looked at her through wary eyes. "How much time?"

"I don't know," she said with a shrug. "However long it takes for us to get to know each other. Become friends."

A snort of laughter shot from his lungs. "Friends."

"What's wrong with that?" she asked, glaring at him.

"Kate," Tom said, giving her a slow up-and-down look. "I've got lots of friends and not a one of them makes me want to strip them naked and carry them off to the forest primeval."

She flushed and he knew it was desire, not embarrassment that put the hot pink color in her cheeks. She might think she could live like a nun, but he was willing to bet he knew her better than that.

At forty-five, he was about to get married, become a father for the second time, and he damn sure had no intention of spending the next year or two living like a monk.

Later that night Tom awoke in a cold sweat, heart racing, pulse pounding. Mouth and throat dry, he swung his legs off the bed and dropped his head into his cupped palms.

Dragging air into his lungs, he reached out and turned the switch on his bedside lamp. Instantly a pool of light beat back the darkness crowding in on him.

"Nightmare," he whispered in a hoarse, choked voice. "Just a dream."

But a helluva dream, he conceded silently. Closing his eyes, he saw it all again clearly. Him. White-haired, trembling, hunched in a wheelchair and being pushed across a grassy field by a young boy in a Little League uniform.

His son. His and Kate's son.

"Jesus," he muttered and let his head fall back on his neck. Eyes wide, he stared at the dark ceiling above him and tried to ease the knot of panic tightening in his chest.

What the hell was he doing?

What the hell was she doing?

Kate stared down at the open file in front of her and tried desperately to concentrate. The list of names and ranks swam in front of her eyes and she swallowed hard as a too-familiar churning in her stomach started with a heavy roll.

She took a deep breath as the neatly printed information swam and spun in front of her eyes. Tiny spots of blackness edged the corners of her vision, and she knew she was fighting a losing battle.

With a choice of curing either the dizziness or the nausea first, she pushed away from her desk, bent over and put her head between her knees. Breathing deeply, evenly, she hoped the faintness would pass in time for her to race to the bathroom down the hall.

Damn it. She couldn't even control her own body anymore. Too many things in her life were spinning out of her reach, beyond her command. And she didn't like it.

Thomas, her work, her stomach.

A peremptory knock on the door, and an unfamiliar voice asked, "Major?"

Kate groaned, too sick to care that someone was about to discover her in a humiliating position.

Quick, light footsteps. A woman then, Kate

thought. The stranger came around the desk and dropped to one knee.

Nice shoes, Kate thought absently, but didn't dare lift her head just yet to see the rest of the woman.

"Are you okay?" her visitor asked, laying one hand on Kate's hair.

"Dandy," she muttered thickly and cautiously, warily easing up into a sitting position. A victory of sorts, since her vision had steadied and the room had apparently stopped spinning.

However, her stomach was still on the offensive.

To get her mind off it, she looked at the woman who stood up and stared at her through concerned eyes. Shoulder-length black hair, brown eyes that looked a bit familiar and civilian clothes.

"Who are you?" Kate asked through gritted teeth.

The woman smiled. "Donna Harris," she said and held out one hand. "Donna *Candello* Harris."

That explained the familiar eyes, Kate told herself as she shook hands with the woman who would soon be her daughter by marriage. Pretty, but more than that, Donna had an open, friendly air about her. She didn't look much younger than Kate herself, and she had to wonder how the woman would take to a stepmother close to her own age.

Blast it, why did she have to be sick *now?* So much for first impressions.

"Sorry about stopping by like this," Donna said. "But I wanted to introduce myself and see if you and Dad would like to come to dinner at our house tonight."

"Your father and I?" Word traveled fast.

"I already asked him and he was all for it, suggested I ask you myself. Don't look so surprised, Major," Donna said on a laugh. "You should know there are no secrets on base."

"True." And she knew that soon people would start talking about just how often Major Jennings seemed to suffer from food poisoning or the flu. She wondered if Donna would be as friendly if she knew that Kate was carrying her little brother or sister.

Lord, she hoped so. She had a feeling she was going to need all the friends she could get in the coming months.

"So, what do you say?" Donna grinned. "I'm making cheese ravioli."

At the words, Kate's stomach soured further. Damn it.

"Major." Donna looked at her warily. "Forgive me, but you look like hell."

"Well, good," Kate told her with a tight smile. "I'd hate to feel this bad and not look it."

'You want me to get a doctor? A Corpsman?"

She would have laughed if she hadn't been afraid to open her mouth that wide. Instead she shook her head. "No, thanks. I'll be fine."

"Are you sure?"

"Yeah. Probably just something I ate."

"If you say so." Donna kept one eye on her as she stood up. "Look, maybe this isn't a good idea for tonight. We can do it another time."

"No." Kate stood up, swallowed heavily and forced a smile. This was important. She wanted

Donna to like her. "We'll be there. It was nice of you to ask us."

"If you're sure..." Donna watched her, and Kate could tell by the look in her eyes that she wasn't doing much of a job covering her nausea.

"What time?" she asked.

"Seven okay?"

She nodded and instantly regretted the motion. "Fine. See you then." Stepping around her desk, she headed for the door. "Now, if you'll excuse me..."

Donna stopped in the open doorway and watched Kate Jennings hurry down the hall. When a staff sergeant walked up to her, Donna only half turned.

"Is the Major all right?"

"I don't know," Donna said thoughtfully, and could hardly wait to talk to her husband about this. She had the distinct feeling it wasn't a bad lunch that had hit Major Kate Jennings so hard.

Six

Tom sat down on one of the two benches lining a redwood picnic table and took a long drink of his beer before throwing a glance at his son-in-law. He'd known Jack Harris for a long time. Had respected him and admired him as a first-class Marine long before his daughter, Donna, had married the man.

And now, since their marriage, Jack had become one of Tom's closest friends.

"Problem, Tom?" Jack asked, propping his elbows on the table.

Off duty, on private time, he and Jack had long ago agreed to a banishment of ranks. Here they were just friends. Family. And whatever was said here would remain here. Tonight Tom needed that sanctuary more than he ever had before.

"I guess you could say that," he admitted, and

looked briefly at the back of the house. Just inside the kitchen, Kate was alone with his daughter. From the sounds of the occasional bursts of laughter, the two of them were getting along great.

And why shouldn't they? he asked himself angrily. The two of them were far closer in age than he and Kate were. He inhaled sharply and blew it out in a rush. Shoving one hand through his hair, he leveled a look at Jack and said, "Kate and I are getting married."

Jack grinned, then slowly, as he eyed his friend more carefully, he asked warily, "Congratulations?"

"Thanks." Grabbing up his beer, Tom stood and walked to the back fence. Leaning his forearms atop the chain link, he ignored the metal barbs and stared off into the night.

From down the street came the sounds of dogs barking. Somewhere a child shouted, a woman laughed and an engine roared. Everyday sounds of life on a busy base. Comfortable sounds. And yet, he didn't feel a damn bit comfortable.

"How about that?" Jack came up alongside him. "A new groom and a grandfather in the same year."

Grandfather.

"Oh, man," Tom muttered as a ripple of cold swept along his spine. Good God, how could he have forgotten that Donna was pregnant?

"Tom?" Jack asked, slapping him hard on the back. "You okay?"

He nodded, still too dumbfounded to speak.

"Why are you looking like you're shell-shocked?"

Jack asked. "Heck. Donna told you about the baby before she told me, remember?"

Yeah. *Now* he remembered. Rubbing one hand across his face, Tom thought back, recalling how his daughter had come to him in tears because she'd thought her marriage was over. She'd told him about the baby and after she'd left his office, Tom had gone straight to Jack and without spilling the beans had read him the riot act.

He groaned inwardly. What kind of man forgets that he's going to be a grandfather? The stupid kind, he told himself. He must have just blacked out the knowledge, being unwilling to admit that he was old enough to be a grandfather. Of course, the fact that Donna had gained hardly a pound and was still wearing jeans had helped in his self-delusion.

So, his grandchild and his new baby would be in the same kindergarten class. He shook his head and wondered if that was some kind of record.

"If you don't mind my saying so, you don't exactly look like the happy bridegroom," Jack said softly.

Tom shot him a look. "To tell you the truth, I don't even know what I'm feeling anymore."

Jack laughed shortly. "Why should you be different from any other man?"

He shoved one hand through his hair and focused his gaze on the moon-cast shadows dappling the base.

"If you remember," Jack said lightly, "I wasn't exactly overjoyed at the prospect of getting married myself."

True. A half smile touched Tom's face briefly as he remembered. Jack had married Donna in an effort to save her reputation as well as Tom's. But it had turned out well, he told himself, taking heart at the thought. If the two of them could start out so badly and end up as happy as they obviously were, maybe Tom and Kate had a chance, too.

The question was, was he up to the test?

He'd done this once before. He already knew he wasn't good husband material. But hell, people could change, right? He was older now. More experienced. More patient. All of that was true, and yet, there was a small kernel of doubt in his guts and it felt as though it was growing.

"So, if you don't want to get married," Jack asked, "why are you?"

"There are reasons," Tom said, unwilling just yet to break the news. He and Kate should decide between them when to start announcing a coming baby. Besides, at the moment, he wasn't entirely sure he could squeeze the words past his throat. "Let's just say they're even more compelling than yours were for taking the plunge."

Jack's eyebrows arched and he gave a low whistle.

"The thing is," Tom muttered, and took another swig of beer. "I've been so busy being supportive I feel like I'm going to explode."

"So explode," Jack told him. "You'll feel better."

Tom snorted a choked laugh. "I doubt it." He stared at the beer bottle in his hands and studied the label as if looking for the answers to his questions.

His son-in-law started talking then and after a few words, Tom tuned him out, listening instead to the tiny voice inside himself.

Married. A new father. Jeez. He was too old for this, wasn't he? The fact that he would soon be a grandfather seemed to prove that point. The nightmares that had become familiar to him over the last few nights taunted him with that sad little fact. And yet…he lifted his gaze again and stared at the dark silhouette of a cluster of eucalyptus trees. Their leaves rustled like dry paper in the slight breeze.

Shouldn't he be looking at this with a bit more wonder?

So what if he and his daughter were both going to be welcoming a baby soon?

Everything happened for a reason. He'd always believed that. So then it had to follow that there was a reason for this child, too. Maybe he should accept this new life as the gift it was and enjoy every moment of it. Maybe his age was a plus here, not a minus.

As a young father, he'd been so focused on ambition and his career he hadn't taken the time to appreciate the little things about fatherhood. Now that his situation in life was different, all of that could change. He could be a part of this pregnancy, this baby's life, in a way he never had been before.

The past couldn't affect him if he didn't allow it to. He could learn to be a good father. Couldn't he?

His brain rushed onward, drawing up images of him touching Kate's rounded belly, then of holding his new baby, pushing it in a stroller. This didn't have to be hard, he told himself. He was very fond of Kate. They could do this and do it well. They could each love their child and still not have to clutter up their own relationship with words like *love* or *forever*.

Words that led to broken promises and shattered hearts.

The tightly coiled spring inside him relaxed for the first time since Kate had sprung her news about the baby. He drew a long, easy breath and smiled.

A baby.

A brand-new chance at life. A brand-new chance to explore the world as seen through the eyes of a child. His smile broadened as the burden he'd been carrying fell from his shoulders. By God, he was going to enjoy this. All of this. He was going to milk every minute of this little miracle and count himself a lucky man.

As for Kate's ''no sex'' edict, he could live with that. For a while. Give her a little time, he thought. Kate was too passionate a woman to live in celibacy forever. Once they'd settled into their marriage, that, too, would work out.

''It's going to be great,'' he muttered aloud, unknowingly interrupting Jack, who was still talking.

Jack slapped him on the back, took a sip of beer and said, ''I'm glad I could help, Tom.''

He turned a questioning glance on the man beside him. ''What?''

Donna and Jack Harris's house was small, typical base housing, but for the two of them it seemed just right. Sitting in the kitchen, Kate let her gaze wander around the tiny room, admiring the little touches Donna had added to make the place seem cozy.

Gingham curtains fluttered over the partially opened window as an ocean breeze danced beneath the glass. A basket of potted chrysanthemums sat at the end of the short counter and from just outside the back door came the soft, tinkling music of a glass wind chime.

The small, round table was cleared of dinner dishes, and a ceramic bowl filled with apples and oranges sat in the middle of it.

Kate curled her fingers around her glass of iced tea and shot a glance at the woman sitting opposite her. Donna hadn't said a word about what had happened that afternoon. But though she'd like to think Tom's daughter had forgotten all about Kate turning green and running for a bathroom, she had to admit the chances of that were slim.

"So you're getting married," Donna said. "That's great."

Kate nodded and smiled. If the smile was a bit forced, Donna didn't seem to notice.

"I knew something was up between you two the minute you walked in," Tom's daughter was saying. "There's almost a—I can't believe I'm going to use the word—*glow* about you guys."

Glow? Probably just cold sweats, Kate told herself, but gamely kept her smile in place.

"I'm glad you're feeling better," Donna said. "You looked horrible this afternoon."

"I remember."

"In fact," Donna went on as if Kate hadn't spoken. "I looked almost that bad myself this morning."

"Really?"

"Uh-huh," she said. "Actually every morning the

past couple of months. I've looked and felt wretched.''

"I'm sorry," Kate told her, and shifted her gaze to her iced tea. Was Donna saying what she thought she was saying?

"Just as wretched as you, I'll bet."

Kate's gaze snapped up to Donna's dark brown, knowing eyes.

"How far along are you?"

Kate's fingers tensed around the glass. She hadn't meant to tell anyone about the baby yet. She'd hoped to wait until at least a few weeks after the wedding, when she and Thomas could announce it together.

"Donna…"

"Don't worry about it," the other woman said and stretched out a hand across the table. "I won't say anything."

It seemed the proverbial cat was out of the bag. "I just don't know how Thomas would feel about my telling people yet."

"I'm not 'people,'" she countered. "I'm his daughter."

"I know, but—"

"Like I said," Donna told her, "don't worry about it. I can keep a secret. Heck," she added with a laugh, "nobody besides Jack and Dad know about the baby I'm carrying."

So she was pregnant, then. To look at the woman in her T-shirt and jeans, no one would guess. Then another thought dashed across her mind, and Kate had to wonder why Thomas hadn't said anything about his impending grandfatherhood. Was he embarrassed to find that his own child would be only a few months younger than his daughter's baby? Oh heavens, this was getting complicated.

"Why aren't you telling anyone?" Kate asked.

Donna shrugged. "People tend to act weird around pregnant people, I've noticed." She took a sip of her tea. "Perfect strangers putting their hands on your stomach, asking personal questions. I'll wait awhile to start dealing with all of that, thanks." She grinned. "Besides, it's sort of fun to have a secret from the rest of the world. Until Junior starts showing," she glanced down at her only slightly rounded abdomen, then laid one hand across it protectively, "he belongs only to us." A soft smile curved her mouth, and tenderness shimmered in her eyes.

A quick, sharp stab of envy pierced Kate's heart. Obviously, Jack Harris had been delighted with the news of his wife's pregnancy. Together, the two of them were entering a special time in their lives, secure in the knowledge of their love for each other and for their child.

Kate skimmed her palm across her flat tummy and silently apologized to the little soul within. This baby should have been greeted with joy, not anxiety. And from this moment on, that's what she would concentrate on. *I promise you.* she pledged silently, *you will be welcomed with nothing but love.*

All she had to do now was convince Thomas.

"I bet Jack's reaction was more pleasant than Thomas's." The words were out before she realized she'd actually said them aloud. After all, Donna was his daughter. She wasn't likely to appreciate criticism of her father. And actually, Kate wasn't in a position to complain, anyway. Thomas had reacted precisely in character. Offering to do his duty and soldier on.

"Was he a jerk?"

Surprised, Kate looked at the dark-haired woman staring at her with eyes too much like Thomas's. "A jerk?"

Donna shrugged and shook her head. "He's really a nice guy," she said, "but he has this tendency toward—" She broke off, sat up straight and squared her shoulders. "Duty, honor and all things stiff and stern."

"He's an honorable man," Kate defended the very man she'd complained of only a moment before.

"Oh, I know," Donna said with a smile at Kate's mother bear attitude. "But sometimes, wouldn't you just like to tell him to lighten up?"

Kate chuckled, shook her head and stood up. She couldn't imagine Thomas being anything but what he was. Besides, she had plenty of memories of Thomas behaving anything but sternly. Although she knew darn well those particular memories shouldn't be shared with the man's daughter. Walking to the sink, she parted the curtains and looked out the window to the back fence where Thomas and Jack were talking quietly.

She knew Thomas enjoyed spending time with Donna and Jack. Here there were no ranks. Only family. Friendship. She wondered idly if even he realized how much he relished being a part of a family.

"So," Donna said on a chuckle as she walked to

join her. "In a few months, Dad's going to be a daddy and a grandfather all at once. Isn't that amazing?"

Kate winced. Amazing indeed. No wonder Thomas had been acting as though he was as old as dirt. Just the word *grandfather* would be enough to shake most men. And a forty-five-year-old man...no matter how virile...would no doubt be twice as susceptible.

Obviously, Kate thought, it was going to be up to her to convince him that a baby would keep him young, not send him to a retirement home. She muffled the sigh building in her chest. It wouldn't be an easy battle. But heaven knew, Marines had been in tough campaigns before. Iwo Jima. Guadalcanal. Anzio.

The trick here, she told herself, was to think of this as The Love Battle. All or nothing. Winner take all. Everything she'd ever wanted was riding on the outcome of her battle plan. Too bad she didn't have one yet.

"He has deeper feelings for you than he admits," Donna said softly, and her words broke through Kate's swirling thoughts and captured her attention completely.

Slowly she turned her head to look at the woman beside her. As much as she'd like to believe Donna, she had to say. "No, he doesn't. Or rather, he won't let himself."

"He can't help it," Donna told her, and laid one arm companionably across Kate's shoulders. "I saw the way he looked at you through dinner."

So had Kate. Instantly, she saw again the fire in his eyes when he caught her looking at him. It was a wonder the tablecloth hadn't spontaneously combusted between them. A low, burning ache settled deep in her body, and not for the first time, she regretted laying down her "no sex" rule. "Oh, he *wants* me," she admitted, then caught herself. This couldn't be an appropriate conversation.

But Donna only laughed. "Why wouldn't he?"

"Wanting and loving are two different things," she said, and turned her gaze again on the taller of the two men standing outside.

"I know that. But there's a shine in his eyes that has nothing to do with lust and everything to do with caring. With love."

Kate shook her head sadly. She wouldn't deceive herself, no matter how tempting. Oh, he cared for her. She knew that. But it wasn't love. Not yet, anyway.

"Look," Donna said. "I know he blames himself for his and my mother's marriage crumbling. But the truth of it is, they were both way too young. Only seventeen, for heaven's sake. They'd only had their driver's licenses for a year. There's no way they could have made that marriage work. Either of them. They didn't even know themselves at that age—let alone each other."

Perfectly reasonable, Kate thought. Donna saw it. Kate saw it. Heck, anyone with half an eye could see it. But Thomas saw only the failure. And it was going to be a long hard fight to help him see beyond that.

"He loves you, Kate. I know he does. He just hasn't realized it yet."

Kate wished that were true. But she was afraid that Thomas's daughter, well meaning though she was,

was too caught up in the glow of her own pregnancy and obvious happiness. She was seeing love and rainbows where they simply didn't exist.

That wasn't love shining in Thomas's eyes. It was honor.

He was going to marry her for the baby's sake. A strong, honorable man committed to doing his duty. Thomas was taking her and their baby on as he would any other burden he deemed his responsibility. Loving him as much as she did, it was heartbreaking to realize that *she* had now become a duty.

Thomas wanted her body. She wanted his love.

Could she one day make him see that what he felt for her was more than desire? Or was she sentencing them both to a lonely marriage where the only thing they truly shared was a love for their child?

"You love him, don't you?" Donna whispered.

Shadows from outside seemed to creep into the brightly lit kitchen and wrap themselves around her heart. It seemed it was the night for sharing secrets.

"Heaven help me, I do," Kate answered softly.

Seven

The drive back to her duplex was a quiet one.

Kate tried to think of something to say. But she kept coming up empty. Mainly because she couldn't think of a tactful way to ask why he hadn't mentioned his daughter's pregnancy. Was he trying to exclude her from his family? If so, this marriage of convenience was going to be doomed from the get-go.

She laced her fingers together in her lap and clenched and unclenched her grip as her mind raced far faster than the flashy truck she was seated in. So much had changed already, and there was so much more to come.

She'd vowed to somehow win Thomas's love, but would she be able to if he was so intent on keeping a distance between them that he wouldn't even talk about his coming grandchild?

Still, she thought, as the truck slowed down, the best way to engage in any campaign was with a strong attack. Winning this Love Battle shouldn't be any different.

When he stopped for a red light just a few blocks from her home, Kate threw caution to the winds and blurted, "Why didn't you tell me Donna's pregnant, too?

He turned his head to look at her. In the strange glow of streetlamps and taillights, his expression tightened, relaxed and finally slipped into a mask of something she'd never seen on his features before. Embarrassment.

"Thomas?"

"The truth?" he asked.

She almost smiled. Almost. "If you don't mind."

His grip on the steering wheel tightened until his knuckles gleamed ivory against his olive skin. "This isn't easy to admit," he told her, wringing the wheel like he would a wet towel. "I...forgot."

Kate blinked. Whatever she'd been expecting, this wasn't it. "You're kidding."

"Wish I was," he said, and added quickly, "please don't tell Donna. First she'd be hurt, then she'd kill me." Shaking his head, he shifted his gaze back to the stream of traffic pouring across Pacific Coast Highway. "I don't see her much now that she's gotten married. And when I do, well, she's not showing yet..." His voice trailed off and he shrugged helplessly. "I don't know, Kate. I just...forgot. Then, too," he continued, shooting her a quick look, "with our news, I've been a little preoccupied."

She smiled slightly. True. Both of them had had plenty to think about in the past week or so. But she had a feeling there was more to his "forgetting" than he was saying.

"Easier not to think about it?" she asked.

"What's that supposed to mean?"

The signal changed, and the cars in the row beside them moved into their left turns.

"A grandfather at forty-five isn't so terrible," she said, and she knew by the way he flinched that she'd hit the nail on the head.

He snorted a choked laugh. "It sure makes me keep a closer eye on the gray in my hair."

Her gaze drifted to the streaks of silver at his temple. She curled her fingers into her palms to keep from reaching up to touch them. "I've always thought that touch of gray very distinguished."

"Yeah?" He turned his head and stared at her, his dark gaze meeting hers. He raised both eyebrows, and a slow smile tugged at the corner of his mouth, deepening the dimple they both knew she was a sucker for.

"Yeah," she admitted.

The driver of the car behind them honked as the light turned green. Thomas turned back to the road ahead, shifted the truck into first gear and stepped on the gas. "Y'know, Kate," he said as he steered the truck into a left turn bay at her street, "by marrying me, you're going to become a grandmother at the ripe old age of thirty-two."

She swayed with the truck as it turned, and felt her thoughts spin wildly, too. She hadn't considered that.

A grandmother and a mother all in the space of a few months time. For a woman who'd lived most of her life alone, thinking she wanted and needed no one, it was a heady thought.

He pulled the truck up in front of her house and shut off the engine. Unsnapping his seat belt, he shifted on the bench seat to look at her. Left arm draped across the steering wheel, his right arm snaked along the back of the seat, almost but not touching her shoulders. Kate fought the urge to lean into him, reminding herself that she was the one who had set the guidelines here. She was the one who had insisted on no more sex until they knew each other better. And though a hug could hardly be called intimate, one touch from Thomas would be enough to ignite a bonfire inside her bright enough and hot enough to melt the strongest resolves.

"So, Grandma," he said softly, "you and Donna seemed to hit it off."

"I like her."

"Good." His gaze shifted past her briefly and a frown flitted across his face. "Your sentry's on duty."

"Huh?" Kate turned toward the duplex in time to see Evie's front drapes swing closed. Obviously her neighbor had been keeping an eye out for her return. "She must think I need protecting," Kate said with a gentle laugh.

"From me?" Thomas's voice rumbled through the close confines of the truck cab and seemed to settle at the base of her spine.

She shivered slightly and felt the weight of his arm

slip around her shoulders. There was no protecting her from Thomas's charms. That little war had been lost three years ago.

"Kate," he whispered as he pulled her closer, "let me come inside." He bent his head to kiss her nape and sent a stampede of goose bumps racing along her back. "Just for a cup of coffee."

"Thomas..." Be strong, she told herself with small hope of success.

"One quick cup and I'm gone," he told her, and shifted his attentions to her earlobe.

She groaned quietly as a too-familiar coil of desire tightened within her. Her fists opened and closed on her lap. Her breath quickened. Her heartbeat stuttered heavily. Blindly staring straight ahead, Kate absently noticed that the windshield was beginning to fog over. Clouds of steam pushed across the glass, blanketing them in a world that was too dangerously private.

"Ah, Kate," he muttered thickly. "I want you so much I can hardly breathe."

Strangely enough, those were the very words she'd needed to hear in order to strengthen her slipping willpower. He *wanted* her. Not love, want.

"Thomas," she said, her voice loud in the stillness. "We can't do this."

"Hmm?" He planted another kiss just beneath her jawline, and she determinedly ignored the rush of sensation that fluttered in the pit of her stomach in response.

Stiffly, she scooted out of his grasp and edged toward the door.

"Kate?" He reached for her, but she eluded his questing hand.

"I said we can't do this, Thomas."

He shoved one hand across the top of his head and leaned back against the seat. Staring at her, he drew in a long, shaky breath. "You're serious about this celibacy thing, then?"

Every instinct she possessed screamed at her to reach for him, wrap her arms around him and never let go. She fought down that urge in the name of her future. She wanted it all. Not just his lust. His love.

And to get that, she'd have to be strong enough for both of them. "This isn't easy for me, either. But we agreed."

Nodding sharply, he said, "I know."

Catching hold of the door handle, she yanked on it, and the heavy door swung wide, letting in a swish of cold ocean air that cleared the windows yet did nothing to cool the fire still raging within her.

"Thomas," she said softly, "I wish—"

"Yeah," he broke in and reached for her hand, giving it a quick, hard squeeze. "Me, too. G'night, Kate."

She nodded, stepped out of the truck and closed the door again. As she hurried up the pansy-lined walk to her front door, she felt Thomas's gaze boring into her back. The intensity of that stare made her knees shake.

As soon as she was safely inside, he fired up the truck and drove away. The echo of the throbbing engine pulsed after him for a long minute and matched the thudding beat of her heart.

* * *

Two weeks later Tom stood at a makeshift altar in his backyard, listening to the base chaplain repeating the sacred vows of matrimony that had been handed down for generations. A cool ocean breeze dusted over the small crowd of guests. He felt the stares boring into his back and tried not to twitch. The collar of Thomas's dress blue uniform suddenly felt about three inches tighter than it had a minute ago.

Maybe the knowledge that he'd made these promises before and had failed to keep them was what had him strung so tightly that he thought his spine might snap. But then, maybe it was simply looking at the woman beside him.

Slanting a glance at Kate, he was amazed again at how calm she seemed. How centered. How blasted beautiful.

Instantly his mind flashed to the moment when Kate had walked down the narrow path leading from his house to the big maple tree where he and the preacher stood waiting.

Breathtaking in a high-collared, pale blue, knee-length dress, she headed straight toward him, her gaze locked with his. Her blond hair was pulled back at the sides and she wore a wreath of roses and baby's breath that matched her bouquet. Winter sunshine played on the silver and gold streaks in her hair and shimmered with a jewel-like light. The small, round bouquet shook slightly in her tight grip, but Tom had a feeling only he had noticed.

Once she had taken her place beside him, though,

her trembling stopped and she'd answered the base chaplain in a strong, clear voice.

She was taking a real chance on him, Tom told himself, and his admiration for her swelled to monumental proportions.

"Colonel?" the chaplain prodded.

"Hmm?"

A muffled titter of laughter rose up behind him.

"The proper response here," the preacher said with an understanding smile, "is I do."

Great. He'd blown his one big line.

Kate looked up at him, and he read the sudden question in her eyes. Good Lord. Did she really believe he would back out on her now? Here?

To erase that question from her or anyone else's mind, he apologized in a loud, deep voice. "Sorry, Chaplain. I was momentarily distracted by the bride's beauty."

Several females in the audience sighed appreciatively.

Kate's gaze dropped, but he thought he detected a glimmer of a smile.

"A completely understandable reaction, Colonel," the chaplain said.

"Would you mind repeating the question?" Tom requested.

As the minister's words rolled out over the crowd, Tom listened carefully to the vows and the inherent pledge lying within. Silently he swore to do everything he could to make this marriage work. To be a friend to Kate and a good father to his child.

Aloud, he said only, "I do," and the deed was done.

A smattering of applause from the twenty or so people attending the backyard ceremony rose up like a hum of bees and settled back down again.

"I now pronounce you man and wife," the minister proclaimed with a flourish. "You may kiss the bride, Colonel."

The bride.

He was a husband again. Soon to be a father again. And this time, by God...he'd do it right.

Tom turned and looked down into Kate's deep blue eyes. If a sheen of water dimmed the color slightly, he supposed a woman had a right to get a little misty on her wedding day.

He smiled at her and was rewarded with an answering curve of her lips.

Married. To a woman whom he respected, liked and admired. How bad could it be? And to top it off, she lit up his insides like a Fourth of July fireworks display.

"Well, Colonel?" the chaplain prodded. "Are you going to kiss her or should we call in the troops for support?"

Laughter rippled out all around them, yanking Tom from his thoughts and bringing him back to the moment at hand. Slowly he grinned. "Thanks, Padre," he said. "I think I can handle this mission on my own."

He bent his head toward her and was inwardly pleased when she went up on her toes to meet him halfway. Lord, he'd missed holding her, kissing her.

It already felt as though it had been years since the last time they'd made love.

Tom meant to give her a brief, chaste, traditional, end-of-wedding kiss, but something happened when his mouth touched hers. Heat blistered the air. His blood sizzled in his veins and his heartbeat jumped into overdrive as it pounded erratically inside his chest. A deep longing hit him with the force of a shotgun blast, and he lost himself in her. As he'd wanted to for weeks.

Their guests, the chaplain, everything disappeared into a hazy background that meant nothing to him. His world suddenly collapsed to contain only him and the woman in his arms.

She moaned gently and parted her lips for him. He invaded her warmth, taking all she offered and silently, hungrily, demanded more. How had he made it these past couple of weeks without the taste of her on his lips? How had he survived the emptiness of not being able to hold her, feel her pressed against him?

This celibacy thing of hers was going to kill him.

At that thought Tom kissed her even more deeply. He held her tight and leaned back, lifting her feet off the ground. She entwined her arms around his neck and clung to him with the same desperate strength that shuddered through him. He felt her need. Felt her desire quicken in time with his and hoped that tonight she would release them both from their vows of chastity.

Oblivious to the shouts, wild applause and the grunted calls of "Ooo-rah!", the bride and groom lost themselves in each other, determined that for the moment at least, tomorrow could take care of itself.

"It was a beautiful wedding, hon," Evie told her and reached up to kiss her cheek.

"Thanks for coming, Evie," Kate said, and meant it. Since she had no family, and her closest friend was presently stationed in Okinawa, the wedding guests had been friends of Thomas's. Except for Evie Bozeman.

True to form, the older woman was dressed outrageously in a lime green, knee-length skirt, topped with a lemon yellow, long-sleeved sweater. And on her feet she wore sneakers.

"That groom of yours looked good enough to eat," Evie commented drily and let her gaze slide over the small crowd until it landed on the Colonel. He seemed to sense her stare and looked their way with a tight and, to Kate's mind, wary smile. "Uniforms just do something to me. Always have. World War II was the best time I ever had—" She caught herself and blushed furiously. "Well, except for all the bloodshed naturally."

"Naturally." Kate couldn't help smiling and was doubly pleased to have Evie there. Lord knew she'd been so busy trying to hide her nervousness all day, it felt good to laugh. To relax a bit.

"So," Evie went on a moment later. "You'll be moving out of the apartment now."

And into Thomas's home. *Their* home now, she thought, letting her gaze slide across the neatly landscaped yard. "Yes, this week."

"I'll miss you, girl."

"You could come and visit me," Kate said, and hoped she would.

"On base?" Evie's silvery eyebrows wiggled dangerously. "Now there's an idea..." Her smile and the speculative gleam in her eye would have worried Thomas.

Music swelled up from the stereo someone had dragged outside and Johnny Mathis's smooth-as-cream voice carried over the muttered conversations.

Kate shot a look at her husband...*husband,* and saw that he was headed toward her, determinedly threading his way through the cluster of people standing on the covered patio. Her stomach skittered and her heartbeat pounded unsteadily. Would he always have this effect on her? she wondered. In twenty years, would she still look into his eyes and feel a slow burn ignite inside her?

"Well," Evie murmured, "looks like you've got your dancing partner. Think I'll just go find one for myself."

In a blink she was gone, and Kate thought she detected a glimmer of relief in Thomas's eyes when he came to a stop directly in front of her.

"I believe," he said, "the first dance belongs to us."

"I'm not a very good dancer, remember?" Even as she said it, she thought, stupid, stupid, stupid. She was the one who had instigated the celibacy rule. She was the one trying to make them find more than sex to bind them together. And what does she do? Introduce the memory of the last time they'd danced together.

In a flash, that night leaped into life in her mind. Candles. Dozens of candles in the Tokyo hotel room. Music drifting through the wall from the room next door and the two of them, doing a slow, careful dance in the shower.

Until she slipped, dragging him down with her in a tangle of limbs that had led to a few very interesting moments.

"Oh, I remember," he said softly and bent to add, "but the floor's not wet here. It should be safe enough." Then he smiled and held out one hand toward her. "Risk it?"

God, she was hopeless. Simply hopeless. One look from those eyes of his and she was a cooked goose. One flash of his dimple and she was a puddle. One touch of his hand and she was a ball of fire, ready to explode.

The memory of their kiss at the altar rose up in her mind, fanning a flame that seemed only too ready to blaze up into an inferno.

Celibacy suddenly seemed like a very bad idea.

But the music played on and Thomas was waiting. She paid no attention to the people watching them. In truth, they might not have been there at all. As she looked up into his eyes, it was as if the two of them were completely alone. Slowly, she placed her hand in his. He moved into the dance, and she felt herself gliding across the concrete patio in a tight, smooth circle. His hand at her waist pressed her tightly to him, and the heat from his palm shot through her to settle down low inside.

She stumbled once, but his strong grip kept her steady, and she knew he would always be there to steady her. Unshakable. Steadfast.

He thought of himself as bad husband material. But he'd entered that first, failed marriage as a child. It was hardly surprising that he and Donna's mother hadn't been able to stay together.

Kate was sure, even if he wasn't, that this time would be different. Now that he'd taken a vow… given his word to be both husband and father, nothing would be able to shake him. She stared up into his eyes and realized that from now on, he would give her everything he could. Everything but his love.

A small twist of pain plucked at her heart.

What if she spent the rest of her life being a duty fulfilled? What if she was never able to convince him that love wasn't a thing to be feared, but to be cherished? What if all they ever would be were intimate strangers?

With that worry bouncing around her mind like a Ping-Pong ball in a box, the music ended.

Eight

"**R**elax and enjoy it, Dad," Donna said as her father led her around the makeshift dance floor.

"I am relaxed," he argued, his gaze shifting from his daughter's face to the crowd beyond, instinctively looking for his new bride. It seemed as though every male guest at the wedding had lined up for a chance to take a spin with the beautiful major.

"Yeah, right." Donna gave his rigid shoulder a shake and laughed. "You're not supposed to be at attention when you're dancing, y'know."

Sighing, Tom gave up the search for Kate and smiled down at her. "Okay, so I'm not relaxed. What groom is?"

"Most of them, I hear, get nervous *before* the wedding, not after."

"I'm a Renaissance man," he quipped. "I do both."

Donna studied him for a long moment, and Tom had the distinct feeling that she was seeing far too much. That hunch was proven right when she spoke again.

"She's really nice, Daddy," she said softly. "If you'll let yourself, you could even be...*happy*."

"Donna—"

"Dad. I know what you're going to say."

"Really?"

"You're going to say that you're no good at marriage and you're scared spitless that you're going to mess up this one."

He gave her a mock frown, trying to pretend that she hadn't hit the mark so effortlessly. "Marines don't get scared, kiddo. You should know that."

"Oh, yeah?" She laughed and inclined her head toward her husband, who hadn't taken his eyes off her all day. "You forget, I'm married to a tough guy. And let me tell you, he's plenty scared at the idea of being a father."

"Tell him to relax," Tom said, giving her a pointed stare. "It'll only be hard on him if he has a daughter who grows up to be a know-it-all."

"A know-it-all who's right, if you please."

Tom shook his head, damned if he would admit just how right she was. What was it about women, anyway? How did they manage to get right to the heart of something?

The music ended and Tom released her, but before she stepped away, she leaned in, looked him dead in the eye and whispered. "Weren't you the man who told me that it didn't really matter how my marriage started? That I could make it into whatever I wanted it to be if I was only willing to work at it?"

Or words to that effect, he thought grimly, recalling the incident perfectly. Damn. Nothing harder than your child using your own words against you.

To Donna he said only, "That was different, sweetie."

"Why?" she asked, again cutting to the center of things. "Because it was me and not you?"

"Donna…"

Another tune started on the stereo, and he took a half step away from her. One thing he really didn't need right now was a lecture from his daughter.

But she stopped his retreat with one hand on his arm. "Dad, all I'm saying is that you have a great chance here. A chance to be happy. Don't blow it because you're afraid to fail."

Before he could say anything in response, Donna's husband came up behind her and claimed her for the next dance. Tom had never been so glad to see the first sergeant. As much as he loved his daughter, he just wasn't up to hearing more advice on marriage from her.

Smiling and nodding at the guests he passed on his way to the punch bowl, he rubbed one hand across the back of his neck and tried not to think about everything Donna had said.

She meant well. But she didn't have the slightest idea what he was feeling. Thinking. She didn't know about Kate's celibacy rule—hardly a recipe for a happy marriage. She didn't know about the baby yet—or did she? he wondered, remembering how much time Donna and Kate had spent together lately.

At the refreshment table, he squeezed in beside a staff sergeant and a captain, muttered a greeting to each of them, then concentrated on the punch. He picked up the ladle, poured himself a cup of the too-sweet liquid and turned, scanning the crowd again, looking for Kate. At last he spotted her in the arms of a newly commissioned lieutenant. Instantly he released every thought, every word and luxuriated in the simple joy of looking at her.

Maybe, he told himself when she laughed up at her dance partner, maybe Donna was right. Maybe with a little effort, his bright new world wouldn't come crashing down around him.

The house was too quiet.

Kate wandered toward the sliding glass doors leading from the living room to the covered patio outside. She met her reflection in the glass, then refocused her vision to stare past the mirror image of herself to the candle-sparkled darkness beyond.

With a sigh, she turned her back on the night and let her gaze slide across the massive living room. The caterers had cleaned and carried away every last trace of the small reception. Only the echoes of the party remained.

Thinking back on it now, the images in her mind were a blur of color and noise. Except for one, she thought. She closed her eyes and brought up the mental picture of Thomas, standing at the flower-bedecked arch beneath the maple tree.

He was tall and gorgeous in his dress blue uniform, and just the sight of him was enough to weaken her knees until she had to lock them and practically goose-step down the short aisle to his side. A wistful smile crossed her face briefly. It could have been so perfect. So wonderful.

Under other circumstances.

If he'd only loved her. But taking vows with a man who was doing his duty…the "responsible thing," certainly wasn't any woman's idea of a romantic wedding.

Glancing down at her left hand, she studied the dull gleam of the burnished gold band on her ring finger. It shone gently in the soft lamplight as she lifted her hand and wiggled her fingers.

It was official. She was married to the man she loved. No going back now. Not that she would want to. But she would give anything at the moment to be leaving on a honeymoon. Instead, she'd be unpacking her suitcases in one of the guest rooms of this big house.

Where she would spend her wedding night.

Alone.

"Kate?"

Thomas walked into the living room, his uniform jacket unbuttoned, hands in his pockets. He looked weary, relaxed and entirely too good.

Resolutely Kate picked up her bouquet from the nearby table and nervously threaded her fingers through the cluster of dark blue ribbons streaming from it. The satin felt cool, smooth, silky. Like Thomas's hair, her mind whispered, and she pushed that thought aside.

"Are you hungry?" he asked. "There's lots of leftovers in the fridge."

Her stomach skittered at the mention of food. "Not very, thanks. You?"

He shook his head and crossed the room to her side. "It was a nice wedding, don't you think?"

It was perfect, she almost said, but settled for, "Beautiful."

"Good of Donna and Jack to stand up for us."

"Yeah," she agreed. "It was." Kate and Donna had already become good friends in the last week or so. And knowing that her husband's grown daughter was on her side rooting for her helped a lot.

"You were beautiful today," he whispered as he came to a stop directly in front of her.

Then the expense of the dress had been worth it. She could have gotten married in her uniform. After all, it hadn't been exactly a formal wedding. But for today, Kate had wanted something purely feminine. Something soft and pretty.

Something to give her confidence in this huge step she was taking.

He lifted one hand and reached out, smoothing back an errant lock of her hair and tucking it behind her ear. She shivered at his touch and told herself she couldn't help it. It was simply a reaction. Like a match to a flame. Fire to dynamite. It simply *was*. Thomas touched her and she trembled.

He let his hand drop, then glanced past her at the

patio and said, "Guess we'd better blow out those candles, huh?"

Kate followed him outside and lifted her face to the soft ocean breeze drifting across the lawn.

They'd barely gone a few steps when her husband stopped dead and half turned to the house again. "Wait a minute," Thomas said. "There's something we should do. I'll be right back." In a couple of strides, he'd disappeared into the house again.

Confused at his abruptness, Kate moved across the cement slab to the first table, bent over the glass hurricane globe and blew out the candle inside. A thin string of smoke lifted into the air, twisted and danced in the wind for a long moment, then disappeared. Sort of like the dreams she used to have about Thomas and her. Thin, wispy imaginings torn apart by reality. She walked along the table, snuffing out two more candles, inhaling the sharp, acrid scent of the burned wicks and pretending that it was the smoke making her eyes water.

Soft, haunting music swelled up out of nowhere and drifted across the patio toward her. She tightened her grip on her bouquet and turned slightly to watch Thomas walk toward her, a bottle of champagne in one hand and two crystal flutes in the other.

God. Evie was right. He did look good enough to eat. And because of her own rules, she wasn't even allowed a taste. That was enough to send a shaft of pure regret slicing along her spine. What she wanted now, more than anything, was to be in his arms. To feel the magic they created whenever they were together. To try to pretend that the lust he felt for her was really love.

This was her wedding day, damn it. And she wasn't going to get a wedding night. The fact that that was due entirely to her was unimportant at the moment.

"I think we deserve a toast, Kate," he said and set both glasses down onto one of the tables still blessed with flickering candlelight.

"Maybe not," she said, despite wanting nothing more than to at least share a toast with her husband on their wedding day. "The baby..."

"A half a glass shouldn't hurt," he said, and poured a splash of the sparkling wine into each glass.

She nodded and accepted the crystal he offered her, running her thumb over the delicate pattern etched into it.

"To us," he said and lifted his flute higher. "And to the baby. May we all be happy." Tom took a sip and watched her over the rim of his glass. She barely touched the wine to her lips before setting the drink down onto the table. A deep, wistful sadness shone in her eyes, touching Tom to the core.

Damn it, he'd wanted everything to be right for her. This was her first...hopefully, her *only* marriage. Her day as a bride. And she deserved to be happy. Lord knew, he couldn't promise much, but he could at least give her today. And maybe, with a little luck...tonight.

"Kate—"

"Thomas," she interrupted him quickly. "It's late. We're both tired. Why don't we just go to bed?"

Those few, simple words set off a blazing inferno

inside him. He looked at her, long and hard, hoping to let her see in his eyes what he was feeling.

Seconds ticked past. Her tongue smoothed across dry lips, and something in the pit of his stomach tightened.

"I mean," she said, after clearing her throat, "you know what I mean."

Yeah, he did. But at the moment he really didn't want to think about going to his empty bed and lying wide-awake in the dark—while she was just across the hall from him.

No, he wanted to hold her, feel her flesh beneath his hands, look down into her passion-glazed eyes and feel the power of the magic that existed between them. He wanted to bury himself in her warmth and feel the silken strength of her arms wrapped tightly around him.

But if he couldn't have that, then he would settle for not letting this night end too soon. "Dance with me, Kate."

She inhaled sharply and took a half step backward, but she bumped into another table and stopped just as abruptly. Shaking her head, she said, "I don't think so, Thomas."

"A dance, Kate." He reached for her, drawing her into the circle of his arms before she could refuse him again. With her breasts flattened against his chest, he held her tightly to him with a firm, gentle pressure. "It's just a dance."

It was much more than a dance, she thought. It was two bodies brushing together. It was electricity arcing brightly. It was want and need and desire. It was everything but love, blast it.

And yet she couldn't pull away.

His arm tightened around her waist. His left hand clasped her right. Her left arm encircled his neck and they danced. The music soared on, strings and horns and the soft ripple of a piano expertly played. He guided her around the patio in a series of slow, smooth turns. White tapers burning beneath the hurricane globes flickered bravely against the darkness and sparkled at the edges of her vision.

Kate looked up into his eyes and let herself believe, if only for this one, incredible special moment, that the shimmer in his eyes was the warm glow of love—not the pale light of duty.

The old, familiar feelings stirred within her.

Her stomach fluttered and her blood sizzled with the heat only he could spark. Caught by the desire in his eyes, Kate felt herself weakening, giving in to the need for him that crowded her days and haunted her dreams.

And God help her, she didn't want to resist.

Strangely enough, it was that realization that gave her the courage to pull out of his grasp and take a much-needed step back. This was a mistake. She couldn't risk being that close to him and still expect to keep from falling into his arms. Her heartbeat racing, her knees trembling, she faced him and whispered, "Don't do this, Thomas."

"Kate," he said softly, "I want to make love with you. You want the same thing. I can see it in your eyes."

"Of course I do," she said, then held up one hand, palm up to keep him from coming any closer. If he took just one more step...if he so much as touched her again, her battle would be lost before it had really begun. "But I also want us to have a good marriage."

"So do I," he said, and shoved both hands into his pockets to keep from reaching out for her again.

"We agreed that a marriage has to be based on more than great sex, Thomas."

"Great sex doesn't hurt, Kate."

"But it's not enough," she said, her voice nearly choking with desire. Pulling in a deep, hopefully calming breath, she went on. "I want more...for both of us...for all *three* of us. Don't you?"

He yanked one hand free of his pants pocket and raked his fingers through his hair. "Naturally, but—"

"Then let's try this my way, all right?" she asked. "At least for a while?"

He shot her a look. "How long a while?"

Everything inside Kate urged her to look at her watch and shout. "Okay, that's enough time, let's go to bed." But she bit those words back and settled for, "I just don't know, Thomas. But we have to try."

He dragged air into his lungs and expelled it in a rush. Gazing up at the starlit sky for a long moment, he seemed to gather himself before looking at her again. Heat still burned in his eyes, and his voice was harsh with strangling need when he said, "All right, then. We'll do it your way."

Instinctively, she stepped forward and laid a hand on his arm. He sucked in another gulp of air as if he'd been branded. She let her hand drop to her side.

"Thanks, Thomas."

Then, before she could lose her nerve, Kate turned and started across the patio toward the house.

"Kate?"

She stopped cold, hoping he wouldn't tempt her again. Hoping her resolve was strong enough to survive another few minutes. Glancing back at him over her shoulder, she asked, "Yes?"

"Yours is the room across the hall from the master bedroom. Your bags are already there."

Across the hall. Just a few short feet of carpet would separate her from the man she most longed to be with. And at that moment Kate wasn't sure who this celibacy thing was going to be harder on.

Thomas…or her?

Nine

Tom woke up slowly, feeling as haggard and tired as he'd been when he went to bed the night before. Dreams of Kate had plagued him as they did every night. Haunting images of her in his bed, in his arms. So real they fed a hunger that couldn't be assuaged, and yet he woke up each morning with empty arms and a heavy heart.

Dragging himself from the bed, he stumbled to the bathroom, turned on the shower and stood completely still, letting cold water pummel his body and force alertness into his eyes. It wouldn't do for the colonel to fall asleep at his desk.

Once dressed for duty, he left his room and groaned quietly as the unmistakable smell of burned eggs reached him. He stepped into the hall and reluctantly turned toward the kitchen. Three weeks of marriage and he'd already consumed enough charcoal to fill a dozen barbecue pits.

Between the lack of sleep and his new wife's cooking, he was in sad shape.

He wasn't sure what Kate was trying to prove, but any time he offered to make a meal for the two of them, she shooed him out of the kitchen like she was June Cleaver or something. Buttoning his camouflage uniform shirt as he walked, Tom steeled himself for this morning's sacrificial breakfast.

Three weeks married and he had to admit that Kate had been right. They didn't know each other well at all. For example, he never would have guessed that beneath her ambitious, career-oriented breast beat the heart of a frustrated homemaker. Not that he minded. Heck, he wanted Kate to be happy. Whether that meant overseeing a battalion or bringing a high-gloss shine to her kitchen floor. He was just surprised, that's all.

And a little concerned about the well-being of his stomach. Rubbing the flat of his hand across his abdomen, he realized that the only time he'd had a decent meal in the past three weeks was when he'd gone to the mess hall. And *that* was saying something.

In his years of bachelor life, Tom had become a pretty good cook. If Kate would only relax a little, he'd be happy to take over the kitchen duties. But she treated the sunshine yellow room as if it were her own private domain, despite the fact that she was a terrible cook.

If it weren't for frozen, microwave meals and hamburger stands, she probably would have starved to death herself years ago.

As he neared the swinging door that separated the kitchen from the dining room, he paused to listen. A small smile crooked one side of his mouth. As usual, his wife was muttering curses at the stove, the pans, the billowing smoke and her own ineptitude.

Now, this Kate, he knew.

Stubborn, determined. Never a woman to know when to quit. That was his Kate. Unfortunately for his stomach, she seemed bent on conquering the intricacies of a cookbook.

He pushed the door open and stepped into what looked like a battle zone. Early-morning sunlight flooded the room, detailing the mess. Flour sprinkled the counters and lay across the tile floor in a wide pattern. Cupboards hung open, dirty bowls and plates crowded the sink, and a tower of black smoke rose eerily from a black skillet.

Kate, a white apron over her uniform, was standing over the trash can, shoveling a pile of what looked like blackened frisbees into the garbage.

He gave a silent prayer of thanksgiving for being spared having to try and chew the disks that were thudding to the bottom of the can.

"What's that?" he asked, almost afraid to hear the answer.

She shot him a look that dared him to comment as she answered, "Blueberry pancakes."

He raised eyebrows and leaned one shoulder against the doorjamb. Studying her, he told himself that it was just his imagination, but she seemed to be getting prettier every day. Even in her uniform she was enough to cause his heartbeat to stagger and his groin to ache.

Dreaming or awake, she had the same damn effect on him.

She sniffed, and his gaze narrowed thoughtfully. "Kate?" he asked. "Are you crying?"

Wiping her eyes with the back of her hand, she shook her head and turned away from him. Disgusted, she practically threw the now-empty plastic platter onto the countertop. "Of course I'm not crying. It would be stupid to cry over a batch of ruined pancakes."

"Then what's wrong?" he asked, ignoring the still-curling spiral of smoke lifting up from where two black eggs rested in the iron skillet.

She laughed shortly, but it was a laugh with no humor in it. Lifting her head, she surveyed the room, then slowly shifted her gaze to his. "What's *wrong?*" she repeated as she reached behind her to tear at the apron strings. "Are you blind? *Look* at this place!"

He had, and it didn't look any different than it had been every morning for the last three weeks. Why she kept beating her head against a stone wall, he couldn't figure out. Even Kate should be able to admit defeat occasionally. But he said only, "It'll clean, Kate. What's really bothering you?"

She snatched the apron off and flung it onto the table. It half landed in a bowl of batter. Groaning, she threw her hands high and let them slap down against her sides. "This. Work. The baby. *You,*" she added, glaring at him.

"Me?" He straightened up and took a step toward her. "What did I do?" Besides try to choke down every last one of her inedible meals. In the next instant she spoke as if she'd been reading his mind.

"You've eaten everything I cook, without a word of complaint." She started pacing, walking a tight circle around the kitchen table, skirting past him without even slowing down. "Doesn't matter how inedible. Doesn't matter how burned. How black and charred. You gulp it down and thank me politely."

Did she think it had been *easy?*

Completely confused now, he gave in to the spurt of irritation riding him and snapped, "Well, hell. Arrange for the execution, Major. Tomorrow works for me."

She stopped dead, spun around and stared icicles at him. God, she was really magnificent. Especially when she was mad.

"Don't you get it?"

"No, Kate, I don't. Explain it to me."

She'd be happy to, she thought. If only she could figure it out herself first. Kate shot a quick glance around the rubble-strewn kitchen and somehow managed to stifle a groan. Every blasted day, she told herself. Every day, she had come into this miserable room and pitted her meagre talents against that damn stove. And every darn day, the stove had emerged victorious.

So far she was losing every skirmish in her campaign to convince Thomas that he loved her. Her battle plan obviously stunk, because she couldn't do something simple like make an edible pancake! Why wasn't she being called on to do something that she was good at? Like score ten out of ten on the rifle range. Throw a grenade. Drive a jeep. Keep hundreds of enlisted men's files straight and at her fingertips.

But, no. This war would be waged in a kitchen. A room that was as foreign to Kate as life in a grass hut on a deserted island.

She'd tried reading recipe cards. At work, she'd talked to some of the other women, trying to understand the mystifying secret of how to arrange for the meat, vegetables and pasta to be ready all at the same time. She'd called Donna for hints on Thomas's favorite foods, but when she'd attempted cooking them, they'd been unrecognizable. She'd used timers and oven thermometers. She'd tried cooking bags and roasting pans. Skillets and griddles. Broilers and barbecues. Nothing worked. No matter what she tried— from grilled cheese sandwiches to a standing rib roast—it always turned into a disaster.

Even the rice that promised to come out perfect every time had defeated her.

A slow simmer of anger built inside her as she lifted her gaze to look at her husband. For three weeks she'd tried everything she could to impress him with her "wifely" skills.

But nothing seemed to matter to him.

He ate what she served him. He wore shirts that she'd ironed—badly. He quietly fixed the vacuum cleaner after she'd broken it. All without saying a word.

Didn't he realize what she was doing? Couldn't he see that she was trying to prove to him how good it was to be married? He seemed to be oblivious to the disasters that followed her around like a big dog on a frayed leash.

Didn't he care at all?

"Thomas," she said, taking a deep breath. "For three weeks, I've been killing myself around here, and for all you've taken notice, I could have been sitting on my rear, eating bonbons."

"What?"

She shoved one hand through her hair, sweeping the mass back from her face. Her stomach twisted, but she fought it back into line. "It's like you're not even here. Don't you even notice what's going on around you? Are you so removed from this marriage that *nothing* interests you?"

"What's that supposed to mean?" he demanded. "Haven't I been here every day? Haven't I tried to help, only to have you push me out of the way?"

"I didn't want your help, I wanted to do it myself."

"Kate—"

His voice was a low rumble of discontent. But she was beyond caring. She'd worked her butt off for three weeks and he'd hardly commented. Now it was her turn. "No, really," she said, beginning to warm to her theme. "You must be able to see that I'm no good at this, but you haven't said a word. Do you just not give a damn?"

"Of course I don't care," he snapped.

She sucked in a gulp of air and jerked her head at him. Well, there was her answer. Hadn't her mother always said, Don't ask the question if you won't like the answer? "Fine. If you'll excuse me..."

She tried to slip past him, but Thomas grabbed her arm, holding her in place beside him. "Why the hell would I care if you can cook or not?" he demanded.

"I'm your wife," she reminded him—unnecessarily, she thought. "Shouldn't that at least interest you?"

"I didn't marry you to gain a cook."

"Fortunately for you."

"Kate, you're misunderstanding."

"On the contrary," she snapped. Every nerve in her body went on full alert. She felt as though she was going to snap in two, and she wasn't even really sure why. Hormones, again? My God, would it never end? "I think I understand perfectly well. You don't care. See? I get it."

His chin hit his chest, and he stood that way for a long moment. Long enough for the grip of his fingers on her arm to begin sending streaks of warmth shooting along her shoulder and down into the pit of her already unsteady stomach.

The tears that were always too close to the surface lately sprang up into her eyes, and she blinked them back. Damn it, she wouldn't cry. No matter what, she wouldn't give in to tears.

Marines don't cry, she reminded herself. Marines persevere. Marines carry on. They damn well do not break down and sniffle.

And certainly not over some lousy blueberry pancakes.

"Kate." He said her name again, but this time,

there was no irritation coloring his tone. If anything, he sounded deliberately patient. As if he was dealing with a recalcitrant three-year-old. "I tried to help with the cooking right at the beginning. *You* were the one who threw me out of the kitchen."

True. But she'd been so desperate to start proving to him how good married life could be, she'd wanted to do it all herself. So much for her first battle plan.

"I wanted to do this right," she said, and hated the whine she heard in her voice. Deliberately trying to mask it, she went on. "Darn it, I hold the record for push-ups in my unit. You'd think I could fry one stinking egg without setting off the smoke alarms."

"That reminds me," he said, glancing around at the still-heavy pall of smoke. "Why didn't they come on this time?"

This time, she repeated silently, sullenly. "Because I disconnected them, that's why. The only thing worse than failure is having trumpets blare to announce it."

He chuckled, damn him, anyway.

One tear slipped from the corner of her eye, and before she could reach up to brush it aside, Thomas did it for her.

One soft, tender stroke of his thumb against her cheek and the tear was gone, replaced by a deeply felt warmth that closed around her heart and squeezed.

"I thought you were doing all of this—" he waved one hand at the wreck of a kitchen "—because you liked it."

She laughed shortly. Liked it? The woman who had spent her entire adult life haunting take-out restaurants and dry cleaners? The woman whose first mission, on being transferred to a new base, was to find a local maid service? No, Kate hated housework. Always had. Mainly because she was so hopeless at it. But she'd so wanted to impress him with her home making skills.

How did other women do it? How did they manage to work and raise kids and keep their houses from exploding around them? And why couldn't she do it, too?

"I hate it," she admitted on a groan, then added, "Oh, Thomas. I'm pathetic."

He laughed again and drew her up close to him. Wrapping his arms around her, he whispered to her bent head. "No, you're not. You're just good at other things, that's all. No shame in that."

Maybe not, but it was hard to see her plan fall apart.

God, but it felt good to be in his arms. To hear his heartbeat beneath her ear. To feel the warm, solid strength of him aligned against her. She'd missed him so much.

Sleeping right across the hall from him was pure torture. Every night, she lay in her bed, alone in the dark, and listened to him moving about his room. If she strained her ears, she could hear his bed frame creak and groan when he lay down, and all she wanted to do was go to him. To join him in that big bed and make the wood frame shriek all night.

But no. *She* had to insist on celibacy.

Another brilliant battle maneuver.

"Kate?" His hands stroked up and down her back,

and even through the fabric of her uniform, she felt the power of his touch. Tendrils of heat, expectation, twirled through her body. Low inside her, she felt the restless, urging need building within.

"Kate—" he said again. His voice rippled along her spine and sent shivers of anticipation darting deep in her abdomen. "I want you, honey. I want you so badly, you're all I think about anymore."

Music to her ears. But how much sweeter it would be if he'd used the word *love*.

She squeezed her eyes tightly shut and inhaled the sharp, clean scent of him. Relishing these few moments in his arms, she had to force herself to take a long step back. To keep her mind on the prize. The future. *Their* future. "Thomas," she said, "I want you, too. I really miss being with you."

He smiled, and that dimple of his nearly did her in.

"Then what are we waiting for?"

How could she tell him that she was waiting to hear him say he loved her? The minute the words were out of her mouth, he would launch into his speech about how lousy he was at marriage. How he'd failed before and wouldn't do it again. How they were better off as friends...*friends!* No, she was in no condition to hear that particular speech again right now.

So she simply said, "Just a while longer, Thomas. I know it's hard, but I think it's important for us to spend the beginning of our marriage getting to know each other as people, not just lovers."

"You're killing me here, honey," he said on a tight groan.

Instinctively she reached up and laid her palm on his cheek. Immediately he covered her hand with one of his, turned his face into her palm and kissed her. She trembled, closed her eyes and savored the touch of his mouth on her skin. It was only after a long moment that she was able to summon the strength to pull free of his grasp.

Looking up into the dark brown eyes that had so captured her from the first, she said, "Please, Thomas. It's important."

He nodded slowly, his jaw tight. "All right, Kate. If it's important to you, then it is to me, too."

It was hard for Kate to know if what she was doing was right when every instinct told her to do something different. But an instant later, something happened that Kate interpreted as a sign that she was on the right track.

She gasped and covered her slightly bulging abdomen with both hands.

Thomas nearly shouted. "What is it? What's wrong? Is it the baby?" Grabbing her arm, he whirled her around and dragged her to a chair. Pushing her down onto it, he knelt in front of her, his gaze locked with hers. "Are you in pain? Is the baby all right? Are you all right?"

"Yes," she whispered, awe pouring through her in a flood of color, like sunshine streaming through a stained-glass window. "We're fine, Thomas. I didn't mean to scare you. It's just that it felt so...weird."

"Weird how? Pain weird? What?" he demanded, his voice harsh with strain. "Should I call the doctor?'' He paused briefly, a look of sheer panic on his face. "Who *is* your doctor?"

"Thomas," she said, and grabbed his hand when he would have turned for the phone. "It's all right, I'm fine. The baby's fine."

He stopped dead, sighed heavily, then dropped to one knee on the floor in front of her. Laying one of his hands atop hers, so that they both cradled the child within her, he said, "What's going on, Kate?"

She waited, holding her breath, concentrating, hoping to feel it again. But when nothing happened, she slowly lifted her gaze to his, heedless of the tears now rolling freely down her face. "It moved, Thomas."

"Moved?" His voice was choked.

"The baby," she whispered, almost reverently. "Our baby moved."

He expelled a pent-up breath, then squeezed her hands gently, still covering her and their child with his broad palm. "Geez, Kate," he said softly, tenderly. "You scared me out of about ten years."

She laughed gently. "Sorry, but I was caught off guard. I had no idea what to expect. Or when to expect it."

"You're about four and a half months now, right?"

"Yeah."

"Then," he said with a smile, "from what I remember, Junior's right on schedule."

Her smile danced briefly across her lips. Then she looked at him through wide, amazed eyes. "He's moving inside me, Thomas. A real, live person, moving inside me."

"I know, baby," he whispered and half rising, he

laid his free arm around her shoulders, still keeping one hand atop her abdomen, helping her caress their child. He rested his chin on the top of her head and simply held her, silently.

"It's a miracle, Thomas," she whispered, still stunned by her reaction to the tiny flicker of movement she'd felt to the depths of her soul. "Our own little miracle."

Her child was suddenly and irrevocably *real* to her. A living, breathing person who would depend on her and Thomas for everything.

And in that moment she vowed to do whatever she had to do to win this love battle she was engaged in. The stakes were high, but the victory would be all the sweeter for it.

Ten

That evening Thomas stole a glance at Kate, across from him, curled up in an overstuffed chair, and not for the first time, realized how glad he was to have her here. His gaze shifted to dart about the room, noting the subtle changes she'd made in his life over the last three weeks.

In the unused hearth stood a brass basket vase containing a huge bouquet of spring flowers. On every chair was at least one brightly colored throw pillow, giving the room a cheerful look even in the dim lighting. A hand-woven blanket that she insisted was called a "throw" was tossed casually over the back of the sofa, and an eclectic array of magazines were arranged neatly on the coffee table.

Small things, he realized, but together they added to the whole, making his house feel like a home for the first time in years. But far more important was that her very presence transformed this place. And him.

Since his marriage, he'd almost been able to forget how quiet this house used to be. Before Kate came, the nights had been long and lonely. He'd wandered through the empty rooms, hungering for the sound of another voice. Smiling to himself, he remembered flipping on the television the moment he entered the door, more for the noise than the entertainment value. Whenever the phone rang, rather than looking at it as an intrusion into his private time, he'd lunged for it gratefully.

But that was then. Now, he told himself, there was Kate. The TV had been on only rarely in the past three weeks. Instead, he and Kate had talked—about their pasts, their jobs, their hopes for the future. And as much as he hated to admit it, Tom had to give her credit. If they'd been sleeping together and had been able to make love every night, as he still longed to do, they probably wouldn't have had this much time to indulge in conversations.

Still, he thought, as he looked her way again, he'd give anything to be able to walk across the few feet of space separating him from her and pull her into his arms. These days, the only time he was lonely was in the middle of the night, when he woke up, instinctively reaching for her.

At that thought his dream images of her rose up in his mind. He dreamed about kissing her. Touching her. Loving her. He spent his days and nights haunted with images of Kate and him locked together in a tangle of sheets.

She sighed heavily, and his idle imaginings were wiped away instantly. "Are you all right?" he asked, and in the stillness his voice seemed overly loud.

"Hmm?" Kate looked up, met his gaze and gave him a half smile. "Yes, Thomas," she said. "I'm fine. I'm just…thinking."

Seemed to be a lot of that going on in this house lately. And he wondered if she indulged her imagination with fantasies of him. Lord, he hoped so. "Not happy thoughts, apparently," he said.

She closed the book on her lap and set it on the table beside her. "Confusing ones, more like," she said, then stood up and walked to the fireplace. She laid her palms on the mantel and stared down at the flowers in the hearth.

He watched her, captivated by the line of her neck, the sweep of her hair and the white-knuckled grip she held on the ledge of wood.

"Thomas," she said, never lifting her gaze from the flowers, "did I ever tell you about my mother?"

"No," he said quietly. Standing up, he walked to her side and, sensing that now wasn't the time to offer comfort, shoved his hands into his pockets to keep from touching her.

Kate shook her head and laughed gently. "She was a single mom." Glancing up at him, she added, "I know I told you that much."

He nodded.

"Well," she dropped her gaze again and continued. "She wasn't very good at juggling her responsibilities," she said. "Worn-out and frazzled most of the time, she gave most of her energy to her job, and I got what was left over." Suddenly she straightened up, released the mantel and turned toward him. "Not that I'm saying she was a bad mother, you understand."

He nodded again, unsure just what she was saying.

"It's just that—" Kate sighed again and pushed one hand through her hair, her fingers spearing through the thick mass. "Maybe some women aren't meant to be the nurturing type. Maybe it's not our fault. Maybe we just lack the right gene or something."

"*Our* fault?" he asked quietly, focusing on the one word in her speech that seemed to define what she was feeling at the moment.

She flinched slightly. "I'm so much like her in so many good ways," she wondered aloud, "what if I'm no good at the parenting business, either? What if I don't know how to do this? What if I mess it up completely?" Turning anguished eyes on Tom, she whispered, "This is a whole new person, Thomas. A blank slate. This baby could be or do anything in the world." Her voice dropped, her bottom lip trembled slightly. "Its future isn't set. It's up to me to make sure it has the best start in life. To see that it feels loved. Secure. It's up to me to give it the kind of life it deserves. What if I fail? What if I'm just no good at loving?" She wrapped her arms around herself and hugged tightly. "My mom tried, you know. She really did. She just wasn't very good at being a mom."

She was serious, he knew. Her doubts and fears

shook in her voice like silken threads in a windstorm. And yet, no one knew better than he did that her fears were groundless.

Warm, giving, kind and tolerant, she was the kind of woman every kid should have for a mother. In the past three weeks, she'd made his house a home, done her job on base effortlessly and had even tried to turn herself into a chef because she'd thought it would please him. If anything, Kate Jennings was *too* giving.

But he knew more than most how old memories could color your future. Wasn't he the one refusing to love again because he'd so ruined his first marriage?

Surrendering to the urge to touch her, Tom pulled his hands free of his pockets and reached for her. Like this morning, she leaned against him, laying her head on his chest, wrapping her arms around his middle. To feel her this way only fed the desire that never seemed to leave him. And yet, for now, he buried that flash of heat in the more pressing need to reassure her.

"First off," he said quietly, his breath brushing the top of her head, "it's not up to *you* alone to take care of this baby. It's up to *us*."

She sniffed and burrowed closer. He smiled to himself, and tightened his hold on her. "And secondly," he went on, "I think your mother did a great job of raising you."

"Oh, yeah, great. Look at me. I'm a mess." Her words were muffled against his chest.

He smiled to himself and rested his chin atop her head. "You're a smart woman, Kate. You know better than to judge yourself based on someone else's failures or successes.''

"We learn from our parents, Thomas. How to be a parent ourselves. If we don't have a good teacher, how good a student can we be?''

He was hoping to disprove that particular theory. But now wasn't the time to voice his own doubts. She needed reassurance here. "On base,'' he said slowly, "you do your job as well as, or better than, any male Marine could.''

"So?''

"I'm not finished.''

"Sorry.''

"In three weeks time, you've made this house into a home...''

She pulled her head back to look up at him through tear-washed eyes.

"And,'' he added, smoothing her hair back from her face, "because of your cooking, I've lost six pounds.''

She laughed shortly and let her forehead fall to his chest. "Perfect. Our baby will weigh seven pounds nine ounces at his high school graduation because his mom can't cook.''

"His dad can,'' Tom reminded her.

"Thank heaven for small favors.'' She shook her head again. "This is all really nice, Thomas, but it's not about mothering. Nurturing.''

"You also have the biggest heart of anyone I've ever known.''

"Thomas...''

"Your mother had it rough, honey,'' he said. "She

was all alone, doing the best she could. We'll have each other and so will the baby."

"Will it be enough?"

"Of course."

"How can you be so sure?"

He was glad she thought so. It meant that he was succeeding at hiding his own fears and insecurities well. Weren't his dreams still haunted by the fear of failing her and his child? Knowing that she, too, was racked by doubts somehow brought his own into perspective. He couldn't afford to wallow in his own anxieties when Kate needed him.

"Because, Kate, if *we* do half as well with our baby as your mother did with you, we're going to have a helluva kid on our hands."

Her lips quirked and his heart twisted. Odd how just a smile from her was enough to ease his soul. Strange how just holding her could bring him a peace he'd never found before her. That train of thought was a little unsettling, so he shoved it aside for the moment.

"So," she asked, tilting her head to one side, "when did you get so full of confidence?"

"It's not confidence, honey. It's determination."

"Determination?"

"To do it right this time," he said and pulled her to him again, needing the feel of her pressed close. "I hardly saw Donna while she was growing up. She came to live with me when she was thirteen and already her own person."

"She's great, though," Kate assured him.

"Yes, she is," he agreed. "Though that has more to do with what her mother did than with me."

"Thomas—" She pulled back again, and he regretted the loss of her pressed to him.

Shaking his head, Tom said, "All I'm saying is that this time, we're in this together, Kate. And together, we'll do right by the baby. We'll figure it out as we go along. Trust me."

"I do, Thomas," she said softly. "I really do, but…"

He grinned. Trust Kate to agree with a condition. "No buts," he told her and smoothed his fingers across her cheek and into her hairline. Gently, he traced the outline of her ear and tugged at the tiny pearl stud shimmering in her ear lobe.

Her breath caught, her eyes squeezed shut and she leaned into his touch. A small part of him was pleased to know that she obviously wanted him as much as he did her. "I've missed you, Kate," he said quietly and heard the longing in his own voice.

"I've missed you, too," she said and took a reluctant step back. "This isn't easy for me, either, Thomas."

Small consolation indeed, he told himself as he tried to rein in the need pumping through him. He looked at her and felt like a starving man staring through an impenetrable barrier at a lavish banquet. A feast for the eyes that left his insides hollow. As empty as his arms.

And he wasn't sure how much longer he could stand living separate from her. Not that he loved her or anything. This was desire, pure and simple. The desire she'd always sparked in him. Every night, as he lay alone in the dark, he told himself that what he was feeling had nothing to do with love.

But every night, it became harder to believe it.

With that uneasy thought in mind, he took a deep breath and announced, "Guess I'll go to bed. Early day tomorrow with General Thornton's visit."

"Oh, no," she moaned. "I'd forgotten about him."

He had to laugh, she sounded so depressed. "He's just going to be looking around, Kate."

"Yeah. Looking to find something wrong."

"Well," Tom said, "if I know you, he won't find anything."

Thomas's words came back to her the very next day as she heard from Eileen about the general's questions. If the man didn't find anything, it wouldn't be for lack of trying.

"He wanted to know everything," the staff sergeant said. "And what I couldn't answer, he got from someone else."

"Wonderful," Kate murmured and leaned back in her chair. Her gaze shifted from one tower of files on her desk to the next. Work was piling up, due to her frequent, hurried trips to the bathroom. Plus, she couldn't seem to concentrate even when she was at her desk, and sometimes her hormones raged so out of control, she'd simply locked herself into her office to indulge in a crying jag that she never would have believed herself capable of. And to top everything off, this morning she hadn't even been able to fasten the waistband of her uniform skirt. Donna Candello might have been able to hide her pregnancy for nearly five months, but apparently Kate wasn't going to be as fortunate.

"Where is he now?" Kate asked warily.

"Down the hall," Eileen said, then shrugged, "but he said he'd be back."

Perfect. Kate's mind raced as she mentally tracked through her work. As she thought, she began to relax a bit, realizing that most of her paperwork was up-to-date and properly filed. Her department was a smooth operation on the whole, and hopefully that would be enough to convince the general that she was on top of things. Otherwise, Kate could singlehandedly give women in the military a black eye.

"Are you all right, Major?"

All right? No. Determined? Yes.

"I will be, Eileen," she said, sitting up and reaching for the nearest stack of files. "If I can whittle down this tower of papers in the next hour or so."

Her assistant grinned conspiratorially. "Would a cup of tea help?"

Kate smiled back. She was almost getting used to hot tea. "Thanks. And keep it coming, will you?"

"Sure." She left, closing the door behind her.

Flipping the first manila folder open, Kate picked up her pen, put her other problems aside and jumped feet first back into the Corps.

"Geez, Kate," Donna whispered, "relax a little, huh? You're more nervous than Jack is."

That's because Jack wasn't giving this little dinner party for a visiting general, Kate thought, and once again let her gaze sweep across the crowded kitchen countertop. They'd had the meal catered, thankfully, so she didn't have to worry about poisoning a superior officer. But she still had to make sure the dinner went smoothly. Not only because she was an officer, but because her husband was the colonel.

Reaching up, she rubbed the spot between her eyes, hoping to soothe the headache beginning to throb there. She'd made it through appetizers and the main course; all that was left was dessert. Then she could crawl to her room and into a hot tub.

"Yoo-hoo, Kate?" Donna's voice came in a singsong fashion. "Are you listening?"

Reining in her racing thoughts was a struggle, but she managed. Glancing at her new daughter-in-law, Kate gave silent thanks again that Donna had attended this little party. Ordinarily a first sergeant and his wife might not be invited, but as the colonel's daughter, Donna most certainly had been.

"I'm here," Kate muttered darkly. "Though I wish I were in Tahiti."

Donna grinned. "It's almost over."

"Three wonderful little words."

"The general's happy, Dad's happy, what's the problem?"

The problem was, she wasn't used to being one of the "wives." She was much more at home chatting with the officers. Now, though, as both a major herself and a colonel's wife to boot, she didn't know which group she belonged to.

Neither and both, she supposed, which didn't clear up a thing for her.

But she didn't say all of that aloud. Instead she only said, "I just want this to go well, that's all."

"Well it is, so cool down."

Good advice. She'd try to take it. Nodding to the enlisted men serving tonight's meal, she went back to the dining room, followed by Donna.

"Ah," the general announced. "Major, I was just telling your husband what a fortunate man he is."

Kate plastered a smile on her face and took her seat. "I hope he agreed with you, General."

Tom shot her a quick grin, and Kate's toes curled.

But the general didn't notice. The older man just went on talking. "You run a tight ship in your department, Major. And you throw a great party."

Relief, pure and heady, washed through her. "Thank you, sir."

"You ever want a change of pace, we could use you in Washington.

Kate blinked and shifted a glance at Thomas. His easy smile was gone, replaced by a quiet, thoughtful look that could almost be described as grim.

But then dessert was served, and the topic of conversation drifted to the Los Angeles Dodgers and their chances for a pennant.

"It was a nice night," Tom said as he turned out the last light in the living room.

"I'm just grateful it's over," Kate told him, and leaned against the doorjamb to pull off her high heels. She sighed heavily, and a small, satisfied smile curved her lips as she luxuriated in the freedom from three inches of torture.

His gaze locked on the soft bow of her mouth, then slipped down along her throat to the deep vee of her red silk blouse. The swell of her breasts enticed him, and he looked lower still, to where his child formed a slight bulge in her abdomen.

He ached to touch her. To trace the changes in her body with his hands. To smooth her skin with his palms and feel her tremble beneath his touch. He wanted nothing more than to slide into her depths and stay there, locked together for the next forty years or so.

"You look beautiful," he whispered, and her eyes opened, darting him a quick glance.

"Thank you," she said softly, then chuckled half-heartedly. "But I'm afraid this will be the last time I'll be wearing this particular skirt. The button's under such a strain, I was afraid all evening it would pop and take someone's eye out."

"I'm sure no one else noticed," he said. At least, no one but him. And Tom found that bulge in her tummy only added to the erotic images his mind formed about her, constantly. Groaning inwardly, he attempted to change the direction of his thoughts. "You impressed the hell out of the general."

Kate grinned. "He liked the strawberry shortcake, anyway."

Tom laughed. "Three helpings worth, but who's counting?"

"Did you notice Jack was too nervous to eat a thing?"

No. He hadn't been paying the slightest attention

to his son-in-law. Or to anyone else for that matter. "All I noticed was you, Kate."

Her breath caught. "Thomas…"

"When the general suggested you move to Washington, I thought my heart would stop. I suddenly couldn't breathe, thinking about being so far from you."

He moved across the room toward her, his path lit by the slivers of moonlight tracing pale fingers along the carpet.

"I'm not interested in going anywhere at the moment," she said quietly.

"Glad to hear it," he said in a rush. "Because I'd miss you. Your hair. Your eyes. God help me, your mouth. Your breasts. Your rounded belly."

She dragged a shaky breath into her lungs and swallowed heavily. "Thomas, I don't think—"

"Don't," he whispered as he came to a stop directly in front of her. "Don't think, Kate. For tonight, just feel."

"Thomas, I only wanted to say—"

He reached up and framed her face with his palms. His thumbs stroked gently across her cheekbones as his gaze moved over her features with deliberate, exquisite, care. "I know what you're going to say, Kate," he told her, his voice a hush of sound in the stillness. "But let me talk first, okay?"

She nodded slowly.

"It's been a long time, Kate. And I need you more than I ever did. I want to hold you," he went on, his body tightening even further as he told her exactly what he longed to do with her. "I want to bury my body inside yours. I want to hear that little surprised gasp you make when we first join together.''

She dipped her head slightly and smiled.

Hooking a finger beneath her chin, he lifted her face until their eyes met. ''Kate, I need you, honey. I need to be with you. I'm so hungry for you, I can't think of anything else anymore.''

''But, Thomas—''

He laid one finger across her lips, silencing any protest she might make.

''Don't make me wait any longer, Kate,'' he said, then corrected himself. ''Don't make *us* wait any longer. Be with me, honey. Be with me tonight. Let's finally and at last, *really* be husband and wife.''

He stopped talking then, because he'd pleaded his case as well as he could. Oh, he might have told her that while the general was talking, Tom had been imagining laying Kate down on the dining room table and covering her with the whipped cream and strawberries just so he could lick it all off her. And he might have said that when he was in a conference with several captains only yesterday, he imagined himself running down the halls to her office, locking her door and taking her there on the floor, surrounded by her mountains of files.

He could even have told her how much he wanted to kiss the swell of her abdomen. To touch the home she'd made for their child and to lavish attention on it and every other square inch of her body.

But he was pretty sure she understood all of that. Knew just by looking at him that he was a man on the ragged edge of desire, and that only she held the key to keeping him whole.

Seconds that felt like hours ticked by. His heartbeat seemed to thunder in his ears. Once again he heard the general's voice, offering Kate a job in D.C. Once again, he felt the floor fall out from underneath him at the very idea of losing her.

Looking into her eyes, he waited what seemed an eternity before she reached up and touched his hair, smoothing a wayward lock from his forehead. Then her small, warm hand caressed the side of his face, and he somehow managed to contain the groan welling inside his chest.

"Thomas," she said softly, a hint of a smile on her face, "all I was going to say was, I want you, too. I don't want to wait another minute."

He breathed again.

"I want you inside me, Thomas. I want to feel like a part of you again."

"Kate," he murmured tightly, his voice strangling in his throat.

Her hands moved to the buttons on her blouse. One by one, slowly, almost as if she was deliberately drawing this out for both of them, Kate pushed the tiny red buttons through their holes until her blouse hung open, revealing a red lace-and-satin bra that nearly brought Tom to his knees.

But even as he thought that, she flicked the front hooks with her thumb and forefinger, releasing her breasts from confinement. The chill air in the room pebbled her nipples instantly and Tom's mouth watered for the taste of her. He looked his fill, savoring the sight of her as a man in the desert appreciates an oasis.

Then she reached for his hands and placed his palms atop her breasts. Arching into him, she let her head fall back on her neck, lifting her lips for his kiss.

"Touch me, Thomas," she whispered from the back of her throat. "Fill me with you, and when we've finished, fill me again."

He kissed her, then, plundering her mouth, taking and giving all he'd longed to share with her for what seemed forever. And it would never be enough.

Eleven

His thumbs and forefingers tweaked her hardened nipples and Kate felt herself melting into a pool of molten desire. Every square inch of her body trembled with the need for more. She shivered in his grasp and parted her lips for his tongue. His sweeping invasion left her breathless, clinging to his shoulders to keep herself upright.

When he moved his hands from her breasts, she moaned her disappointment, but it was short-lived. He bent and scooped her into his arms, cradling her close as he hurried down the hall to the master bedroom.

Kate didn't even glance at the guest room where she'd been staying for the past three weeks. Tonight that was over. She couldn't wait another day. Couldn't bear the thought of spending one more night apart from him.

The darkened room was awash with moonlight, its dim, silvery glow splashing across the wide bed and its dark blue quilt. Striding toward the bed, Thomas set her on her feet, then reached down and grabbed the quilt, tossing it to the foot of the mattress.

Trembling, Kate shrugged out of her blouse, then let her bra slide down her arms to fall on the floor at her feet.

He pulled in a long breath and released it on a sigh. Reaching for her, he laid both hands atop her breasts again, rubbing his palms across her nipples until Kate swayed unsteadily, bracing the backs of her knees against the bed.

"It's been a long time, Kate," he murmured, then bent his head to kiss first one erect, dark pink nipple, then the other.

She moaned and clutched at the back of his head. "Too long, Thomas. Far too long."

He smiled against her, she felt his lips curve. Then he straightened and looked down at her. His dimple flashed, and Kate's stomach flip-flopped. "We've been married nearly a month, Kate."

She didn't know where he was going with this, and at the moment, she didn't care. Reaching for the buttons of his long-sleeved white shirt, she hurriedly undid them, anxious to have the feel of his skin beneath her hands. But when his chest was bared, he caught her wrists and held them tight.

"Thomas?"

He smiled and shook his head. "As much as I want to just toss you onto this mattress and join you there, I'm going to take my time about this."

She almost groaned. All she wanted now was him. His touch. His body.

"A month married or not, Kate," he said softly, drawing her gaze up to meet his, "this is our wedding night." Then he grinned again. "And it's going to be a long one."

She shivered in anticipation, even as his words tugged at her heart. He did love her. She knew it. She could feel it. Why else would a man tormented by desire want to take his time and make this night as special as it should be?"

"Whatever you say, Colonel," she whispered through suddenly dry lips.

"Someday, I'm going to remind you of those words," he teased, then gave her just enough of a push so that she lost her balance and flopped backward onto the bed. "But for now, I'm through talking."

"Thank heaven," she whispered, and held her arms up to welcome him.

Instead of joining her, though, Thomas slowly undressed, tossing his clothes heedlessly into a pile. Kate watched his every move, luxuriating in the pleasure of seeing his magnificent body again after so long. She reached for him, wanting to stroke the finely muscled, tanned flesh of his chest, but he kept out of reach, that damned dimple of his teasing her.

When he was naked, he turned his attentions to her. Carefully, he slid her skirt off, drawing it down over her hips and along her legs, leaving her in nothing more than a half-slip, her panties, stockings and garters.

Deep inside her, Kate's muscles twitched eagerly. A damp warmth flooded her, pooling in her center, aching for his attentions. But Thomas wouldn't be rushed.

He tugged her black silk slip down and off, then paused to admire the picture she made against the soft, white sheets. ''Kate, if you only knew how often I've imagined you here, just like this...''

Even though she'd known that was true, her heart soared to hear the words. If she missed hearing three more little words, she told herself that at this moment, it didn't matter to her. All that mattered was finding what she'd had with Thomas again. Finding the magic they always discovered when they were together.

''Thomas, I want—''

She broke off when he hooked his fingers beneath the band of her panties and pulled them down. Sensations crowded one on top of the other. She felt the cool of the sheets beneath her back, the chill air dusting across her most-sensitive flesh and his fingertips along her calves, branding her with the heat of his touch.

Swirling tendrils of expectation rose up inside her as his hands moved slowly, inexorably up the length of her legs. Her calves, the backs of her knees...Kate sucked in a breath when his fingertips dusted across her skin in just the right places. And then up farther still. He bent over her, running his palms lightly, teasingly along the outsides of her thighs and up to her hips, covered now only by the lace of her garters.

''Oh, my,'' she whispered brokenly, giving herself over to the churning emotions boiling within.

Thomas. Only Thomas. His fingertips slid across her flesh, beneath the garters and around to the insides of her thighs. Through the filmy fabric of her silk stockings, his hands worked a magic that threw her into a maelstrom of feelings.

She parted her legs, silently offering him more, demanding more from him. Kate thought she heard him chuckle, but she couldn't summon the strength to open her eyes and check. Every ounce of her being was focused now on the placement of his hands. On willing his fingers to move a bit higher. To touch her center. To stroke the tender spots within her that would bring her to the edge of eternity and back again.

And then he did and Kate gasped.

Gently, tenderly, he stroked her most-intimate flesh, building the fire that threatened even now to engulf her. Over and over again his fingertips danced across her body, rubbing, caressing, touching her in the way that only he ever had. He slipped one finger into her warmth, and Kate felt as though she might catapult right off the bed. Instead, she grabbed handfuls of the sheet and held on tight to a world that was suddenly spinning out of control.

"Let go, Kate," he said, "let me watch the pleasure take you."

Her breath came in short, harsh gulps. A spiraling sensation built low in her belly and threaded upward, sending ribbons of delight streaming throughout her bloodstream. Still, she fought the release hovering just out of reach, wanting to make this heavenly torture last for hours. And when he stopped touching her, she thought she might weep for the loss of him.

"Thomas..."

"It's all right, Kate," he whispered, "just slide down here." He took hold of her legs and pulled her toward the edge of the mattress. She lifted her head to look at him and when she figured out what he had in mind, she groaned in anticipation.

Kneeling on the floor, Thomas set her legs across his shoulders, letting her feet dangle against his back. Smiling up at her, he smoothed his palms across her skin, pushing over the small bulge in her abdomen, then sliding down to cup her behind.

"Oh, Thomas," she said, "you don't have to—"

Then his mouth closed over her and she forgot to breathe. His lips and tongue smoothed over her center, nibbling, licking, teasing, torturing her with adoration. Kate raced toward completion now, unable to withstand such intimate attentions. Lifting her head slightly, she looked down at him, watching him love her. Watching him take all she was and give her even more in return.

As the first wave of release hit her, Kate called his name brokenly. Her hips rocked. His hands on her bottom tightened their hold, and, safe in his grasp, she plummeted into the abyss that had been waiting just for her.

No sooner had the convulsive easing passed, than Thomas raised up on his knees and bent over her still-quivering body. Tears filled her eyes as the man she loved kissed the swell of their child.

"Happy wedding," he said with a wink.

"This is your wedding night, too," she reminded him, touched deeply by his tenderness. "It shouldn't all be for me, Thomas."

Smiling as he shifted her gently to the middle of the bed, he assured her. "Believe me, Kate. It was my pleasure." As he positioned himself between her thighs, he added, "And so is this."

Pushing himself into her depths, Tom paused to savor the moment of coming home. Because that was what it felt like. Entering a safe harbor. Going home, to a home he'd always longed for. Kate. It was always Kate. There was magic here, he knew. He supposed a poet would call it love. But a man burned by that emotion could only call it peace.

She gasped lightly, and he smiled to himself. That was the sound he had so craved to hear. And as her legs came around his waist, pulling him closer, deeper, he stopped asking himself what it was he was feeling and only felt grateful that he'd found it again.

Dipping his head to claim a kiss, Tom gave himself over to the sensations pouring through him. Locked inside Kate's body, he relentlessly pushed them both higher and higher until the only way to find release was to plunge together off the edge of the precipice.

And when they fell, they were safe in each other's arms.

Sated and secure in the crook of his arm, Kate knew that it was now or never. She'd already changed her battle plan, although she could admit now that it had never been a very good one. How could withholding love—even physical love—teach a man *how* to love?

No, she told herself as she listened to the steady beat of Thomas's heart beneath her cheek, the only way to fight the war for his love was to use the right ammunition. Why shouldn't she profess her love for him? Why should she pretend to be something she wasn't?

Maybe, if he heard her say the words often enough, he would eventually come to believe in them and actually say them himself. Surely any man confronted with love, there for the taking, would see that it was a good thing. Something to cling to and cherish, not to hold at arm's length.

So, she'd shift battle plans again and use her love as her most powerful weapon. Day by day, night by night, she would eat away at his defenses. Until finally he would understand that love would make him—*them* stronger.

Running the flat of her hand across his chest, she whispered hesitantly, "Thomas—"

He gave her a brief, tight squeeze. "Please don't tell me you think we should go back to separate bedrooms, Kate."

"Not at all," she said quickly, levering up on one elbow to look down at him. Never again, she thought. If she was to convince him to love her, she would need every bit of ammo she could get. Especially sharing a bed with him. "I just wanted to say something."

He looked up at her, and Kate's heartbeat staggered with the strength of her love for him. She could survive without him, she knew. But it would be only that. Survival. She wanted more for herself. For her baby. For him.

She wanted life. And love. With a capital *L*.

With that thought firmly in mind, she took a deep breath and blurted out the truth she'd hidden from him for three long years. "I love you, Thomas."

Instantly a shield went up across his eyes. She watched him stiffen, watched his features tighten, and spoke again quickly, before he had a chance to erect barriers too fierce to breach.

"I'm not asking to hear the same thing from you," she told him and added silently, *not yet, anyway.* "I just wanted you to know."

"Kate," he said, his voice low, deep and careful. "I've already told you. Love is just not something I'm good at."

You're wrong, she said silently. So wrong. Couldn't he see how he was with her? With Donna? Was the man so blind as to think that one failure destined him to a long series of the same? She wanted to shake him, but knew it wouldn't do any good. Instead, she said, "I think you're wrong, Thomas. But it doesn't matter what I think. You're the only one who can decide to let love be a part of your life."

He inhaled deeply, as if preparing to defend himself, but Kate spoke up quickly, cutting him off before he had a chance to say anything.

"I love you," she repeated. "That love doesn't cost you anything. Doesn't depend on you for anything. Doesn't come with a list of requirements. It just *is*."

"Kate, honey, why are you saying this now?"

"We're married, Thomas. We're going to have a baby. And I wanted you to know that I love you." It felt good to finally say the words, even though she would have dearly loved to hear them in return. For now, it had to be enough that she loved him and he knew it.

Snuggling down beside him, she laid her head on his chest and smiled when his arms came around her. But her smile faded slightly a moment later when he whispered. "Love wasn't part of our bargain, Kate."

"Bargains change, Thomas. People change." In fact, she was betting their future that *he* would change. That he could learn to accept love as the greatest gift.

He sighed heavily and ran one hand across her hair. "I can't promise to love you, Kate. But I swear I'll do my best by you and the baby."

Her heart breaking just a little, she murmured, "I know you will, Thomas. I know."

"Don't give up on him, Kate," Donna said. "He's worth the fight."

Kate gripped the telephone tightly and said, "I know, Donna. It's just that—"

"He's hardheaded, but he's not stupid."

Kate smiled and reached for her pen. Doodling on a notepad while Donna talked, she wasn't even surprised to find herself drawing little circles that wrapped around and around each other. It seemed to sum up her life lately. Ever since she'd confessed her love to Thomas, she'd been spinning in circles.

On the surface, nothing had changed in their marriage but her bedroom. Now she spent every night in Thomas's big bed. Her body was well loved, but her soul was starving to death.

Damn his stubbornness. She *knew* he loved her. She felt it when he touched her. Heard it in his voice. But without the words, a piece of her heart died a little every day.

"Look," Donna was saying now, "he's a good guy, Kate. And whether he's willing to admit it or not, he does love you."

"The key is, he won't admit it." She shouldn't be discussing this with the man's daughter, for heaven's sake. She hadn't meant to get drawn into this conversation at all. But there was something about Donna that invited confidences.

"He will, you'll see." A long pause, and then she said, "I've never seen him this happy, Kate. Not with my mother. Not with anyone. And he deserves happiness as much as you do."

"Thanks."

"If you'd like, I could ask Jack to talk to him—"

"Good heavens, no!" Kate sat straight up. The one thing she didn't want right now was for Thomas to know she was talking about him with Donna.

"Just as well. Jack probably wouldn't do it, anyway."

"Look, Donna," Kate said and glanced up when her adjutant opened the door. Motioning Eileen to wait a minute, she lowered her voice and said, "I know you're trying to help, but really…don't do anything. Okay?"

"Okay. I won't."

"Thank you. I've gotta go, so—"

"I'll call you later in the week. Maybe we could take in a movie."

"Sounds good. 'Bye." She hung up, then looked at Eileen. "What is it?"

"A letter for you. From Washington." Eileen's eyebrows lifted. "From General Thornton's office."

"Thanks," Kate said, holding one hand out for the letter. When she was alone again, she slit the envelope, pulled out the single typed page and read.

"Major Candello, This letter is to restate my offer of a position on my staff. If you're interested, please contact me and we can start working on the transfer papers." It went on another paragraph or two, but the heart of the matter was simple. She'd been offered a prestigious job on a general's staff.

Kate leaned back in her chair. Her career could take a fast leap here. This could lead to everything she'd ever worked for. Even a year ago she would have dropped everything in an effort to accept the general's offer.

But just a year ago her career was all she had. That and a once-a-year tryst with Thomas. Now though… her gaze dropped to her abdomen and then to the gold band on her left hand.

There was so much more in her life than just furthering her career. There was family. There was love.

Wasn't there?

Thoughtfully, she folded the letter and slipped it into the top drawer of her desk. She didn't have to answer it right away. General Thornton hadn't put a time limit on his offer. But she couldn't help wondering what Thomas would say when—if she told him about it.

If?

No, she wouldn't tell him. Not now, anyway. No sense talking about something that might not happen.

A week later Tom was still mulling over Kate's confession. Though something inside him rejoiced to know that she loved him, there was another part of him that was simply terrified.

And sitting in the obstetrician's office wasn't helping anything.

He glanced around at the others in the tiny, pink-and-blue waiting room. He was the only man present. Kate had tried to tell him he didn't have to go to her appointment, but Tom was adamant. This time around, he was going to do things right with his child from the beginning. Including his first ultrasound.

Leaning forward, he flipped through the magazines scattered across the low table, *Parenting, Single Parenting, Breast-Feeding, Baby and me.* Feeling more and more out of place, he selected one blindly and opened it to a particularly intriguing article entitled "The Scoop about Poop."

Rolling his eyes, he tossed the magazine down and leaned back in his chair, crossing his hands over his middle. One of the pregnant women gave him a shy smile.

"Your first?" she asked.

"No, second," he answered, not feeling it necessary to point out that his first had been born twenty-some years before.

She rubbed one hand over a belly that looked as though it was about to pop and smiled tenderly. "She's my first. I wish my husband had come with me. Your wife is a lucky woman."

Tom doubted if Kate thought so at the moment. Despite what she said to the contrary, he knew damn well she would like to hear him say, *I love you*. He only wished he could.

But it had been too long. He was too old now to take that particular risk again. Wasn't it enough that they were married? Having a baby? Even as he asked himself those questions, he knew the answer. No. It wasn't enough.

Kate deserved better.

He only wished he could give it to her.

The door to the inner office swung wide and a too perky nurse peeked her head out. "Colonel Candello?"

He leaped to his feet.

"At ease, Colonel," the nurse said with a smile. "You can come in now. The show's about to start."

As he headed for the door, the young woman behind him said, "Good luck!"

"Thanks," he answered, knowing he'd need all the luck he could get in the coming months.

Kate lay stretched out on the examining table, her white paper gown pushed up under her breasts, exposing an abdomen that had been coated with some kind of gel. Beside what looked like a small television set, the doctor sat on a swiveling stool. Seeing him enter, she swung her long hair out of her way and said, "Come on in, Dad. We've been waiting for you."

Tom shot a look at Kate's anxious face and hurriedly crossed the small room to her side. Giving her a tight smile, he took her hand and didn't even wince when she squeezed it, hard.

"I'm glad you came, Thomas," she said softly.

"Wouldn't have missed it," he told her honestly. Amazing how things had changed since the last time he'd become a father. Now it was routine to know the sex of your child before its birth. Routine to peek into its prebirth world.

Someone turned off the lights and the show started.

Tom's stomach did a sudden, unexpected flip-flop and he held his breath, as entranced as Kate by the developing images on the screen.

Doctor Hauck wielded the ultrasound wand herself, smoothing the plastic device back and forth across Kate's stomach. Tom found himself squinting at the gray screen, not really sure what he was looking for. They hadn't had these gizmos the last time he'd been an expectant father. Or at least, if they had, he hadn't been aware of it.

But then, he recalled sadly, he hadn't been aware of a lot of things.

"There she is," the doctor crowed.

"Oh my," Kate whispered, giving his hand another squeeze.

"She?" Tom asked, squinting harder. How did they see these things?"

"All of my babies are *she's* until proven otherwise," the doctor told him with a chuckle. "And I think we're about to find out the answer to that little mystery. See how she's turning?"

Where? Tom thought, narrowing his gaze farther as he tried to make sense of the images on the screen.

As if she'd heard his thoughts, the doctor reached up and with her index finger, traced the outline of his child.

"There's her head and her arms and legs and—"

His mouth went dry. His baby. Right there for everyone to see. Amazing. The secrets of life, always hidden from mere men were all of a sudden out in the open. He felt blessed in a way that he'd never expected. And somehow, humbled by the miracle that was playing out right in front of him.

"Oops," Doctor Hauck announced, "excuse me, everybody! Make that *his* head, *his* arms and legs..."

"A boy," Kate said with wonder.

"Definitely," the doctor said, laughing.

"A son," Tom whispered the words, a bit awe-struck. Though he would have been just as pleased with a daughter, a boy would be fun, too. He had a daughter. He'd experienced first dances and boy-friends and marathon telephone sessions. Now he would get a chance to experience the other side of the spectrum.

Instantly images of Little League games, baseball caps and marbles floated in front of his eyes. He could almost see the child, with Kate's shining blue eyes and wide smile.

He continued to watch the screen, marveling at this first movie of his child. Then his gaze focused on one specific area. "What's that pulsing thing there?" he heard himself ask.

Doctor Hauck turned toward him. Smiling gently, she said, "That, Colonel Candello, is your son's heart beating."

His eyes widened as he stared at the image on the screen.

If someone had punched him in the stomach, he couldn't have felt the hit harder. Wonder filled him. A film of unexpected tears sheened his eyes. He struggled to draw air into his lungs as he tore his gaze from flickering images long enough to look down at Kate.

She looked as thunderstruck as he felt. Not even surprised to find a tear streaking along her cheek, he smoothed it away with the pad of his thumb. Then he bent down low and whispered in her ear, "Thank you, Kate. Thank you for this moment."

"I love you," she said just as quietly.

And somehow, hearing those words now, felt right.

"I know," he said, awed as much by her as by the sight of his unborn child.

Twelve

Days became weeks, and the weeks swiftly turned into months. Time was slipping by, and Kate was no closer to claiming Thomas's love.

Feeling the need to talk to someone, Kate found herself at Evie's house. Leaning against Evie's porch railing, Kate sighed. Oh, Thomas was caring, kind and considerate. They shared the chores at home, although he did most of the cooking now. They went for long walks, discussed baby names, indulged in tentative plans for their son's distant future and shopped for baby clothes and furniture.

He accompanied her to all of her doctor's appointments. He bought a copy of every parenting book he came across and had signed them both up for Lamaze classes. In fact, ever since that first ultrasound, he'd shown nothing but enthusiasm for the coming baby.

In short, he was the perfect father-to-be.

That should make her happy, she knew.

Instead, Kate found herself wishing Thomas would feel for her just half of what he was feeling for the baby. Embarrassing...and sad, to admit to almost being jealous of your unborn child.

Kate's hand dropped to her well-rounded belly as if apologizing for her thoughts.

"Baby kicking?" Evie asked gently.

"No," she answered, glancing at her former neighbor and landlady. "It's not the baby, it's me."

"Whatever could be bothering you on such a glorious day?" the older woman asked as she poured two glasses of iced tea.

Kate stared out across the lawn, noting absently that Evie had added one or two plaster gnomes to the menagerie dancing across the recently mowed grass. The pansies along the walkway dipped their colorful heads in a soft breeze, and the sunshine reaching the porch where they sat was dappled and softened by the vivid, purple blooms of a giant jacaranda tree.

It really was a beautiful day. Too beautiful to feel as wretched as she did. But it was damned hard to maintain a happy face when faced with the growing knowledge that your husband was never going to love you.

Her lips twisted as the too-familiar ache in her heart blossomed.

"Honey," Evie said, reaching out to pat one of Kate's hands. "What is it? What's wrong?"

"Only everything," Kate muttered, then flashed the older woman a wry smile. "Sorry you asked?"

Evie's features softened into an expression of quiet understanding. "Not a bit," she assured her. "I wouldn't have asked if I didn't want to know." Picking up one of the green glass tumblers, she handed it to Kate and said, "Take a sip, then spill your guts."

Kate blinked.

"Metaphorically speaking, of course," Evie told her with a smile.

"I don't even know where to start."

"Start wherever you want to, then skip around to fill in the blanks."

She did need to talk to somebody. Kate couldn't very well go to Donna with her worries. Not only did the woman have enough to think about, being only a few weeks further along in her pregnancy than Kate, but Thomas *was* her father.

So she had come to Evie. The older woman had always struck Kate as a very practical, common sense kind of person. And right now, she could use some advice.

Setting her iced tea down on the glass-topped table beside her, Kate took a deep breath and started talking. And when she was finally finished, Evie leaned back in her chair and stared at her thoughtfully. "You do have a problem or two, don't you?"

"And I'm running out of time, Evie." Kate jumped to her feet and walked into the yard. Restless, uneasy, she needed to move. To be doing something. The soft, sun-warmed grass felt good on her feet. She tipped her head back to stare up at the profusion of purple flowers above her and watched as the wind plucked tiny, horn-shaped blooms and sent them flying across the yard to lie in a lavender carpet on the lawn.

"The baby will be born in just a little under two months I can't keep waiting, hoping that Thomas will wake up and realize that he loves me." She glanced at Evie as the woman walked up to stand beside her. "And I can't bear the idea of raising a child in a house where love is considered unimportant."

"So what are you going to do?"

"I don't know," she admitted, and that was the hardest part of all of this. She'd tried everything she could to reach Thomas. "I went into this marriage determined to wage a successful campaign."

'Ah." Evie said and nodded. "A military mind at work."

A bit defensive, Kate looked at her and said, "It's what I know, Evie. It's who I am."

"Of course," she replied.

She didn't seem convinced, though, so Kate added, "I systematically went about wearing down his defenses."

"So why didn't it work?"

Why indeed? "Apparently his defenses are more fortified than I'd thought."

"Maybe you're going at this the wrong way, honey," Evie ventured.

"What do you mean?"

A gentle breeze ruffled Evie's silvery hair and lifted the collar of her bold red-and-green soccer jersey. "Think about it," she said. "What have you done in the past three months?"

"Nothing extraordinary." Kate shrugged. "Went

to work. Came home. Spent time with Thomas. Went to doctor's appointments.''

"Ah," Evie said, wagging her index finger at Kate. "You see, *that's* where the mistake comes in."

Frowning, Kate looked down at her friend in confusion. She didn't understand and said so.

"What I mean is, you've given Thomas everything the man could want, right?"

"I suppose," she said, not quite sure where the other woman was headed with this.

"Of course you have!" Sniffing, Evie went on, a dangerous gleam in her eye. "You're a career woman, good at your job."

"Yeah…"

"You're a wife, home every night, sharing the household tasks."

"Uh-huh…"

"You're carrying his child—a *son,* no less," Evie held up one hand for silence as Kate started to interrupt. "Say what you will, a man wants a son. Oh, it's not politically correct these days to admit to such a thing, but that doesn't make it untrue."

"Maybe…" But Kate wasn't convinced. She'd seen Thomas's face the day of the ultrasound. Tears stung the backs of her eyes at the memory. He'd been awestruck by the miracle long before the doctor had told them the baby's sex.

"At any rate," Evie continued, demanding her attention once more, "the man has it made in the shade."

"Evie…"

The older woman held up one hand and ticked off

her reasons on her fingers. "A smart career woman. A wife. A mother. A warm and welcoming lover."

Amazingly enough, Kate felt the stirrings of a blush steal up her neck. For heaven's sake.

"And to top it all off, you always let him know that you love him, don't you?"

"Well, naturally," Kate said. "That was the whole object of my battle plan. To get him to the point where he not only was used to hearing me say those three little words, but actually *enjoyed* it, too."

"And does he, do you think?"

"I think so," she said after a moment's thought. There was no more of the trapped animal in his look when she professed her love. More of a pleased acceptance.

"Well, why shouldn't he?" Evie threw her hands high in the air, then let them slap down along her sides again. Clearly exasperated with her, she stared at Kate for a long moment before asking, "Don't you see?"

"No. See what?"

"You've given him what he needs without asking for anything in return. Why shouldn't he be happy?"

A bubble of irritation rose up inside her and she batted it back down. "If I have to *ask* for his love, it won't mean anything."

"Hogwash."

"Huh?"

Evie shook her head. "I've said it before, and I'll say it again. Youth is wasted on the wrong people." Taking a deep breath, she continued just as hotly, "If Thomas came to you and said, 'Tell me you love me,

Kate,' would his asking to hear it devalue what you feel for him? Make it worthless?''

''No.'' Ridiculous question.

''So why do you think it would devalue his declaration for you?''

Kate opened her mouth to explain just how it was different, but couldn't. Pressing her lips together tightly, she realized that Evie was right. About everything. Thomas hadn't confessed his love because Kate had let him know that she was willing to go on as they were forever.

Why *should* he take the last leap of faith? She'd as much as told him he didn't have to.

''I'm an idiot,'' she whispered, shaking her head.

''Not an idiot,'' Evie assured her with a chuckle. ''Just a woman in love trying to do the right thing for everyone involved. The only problem is, dear—''

Kate looked at her.

''You've been looking after everyone but yourself. You're careful of Thomas's feelings. Watching out for your baby, and those are good things. But you're important, too, honey. And it's time you took a stand.''

''Maybe you're right,'' Kate said softly, shifting her gaze to stare off into space.

''Of course I'm right,'' Evie told her. ''Ask anyone. They'll tell you I'm *always* right.''

Ignoring that particular statement, Kate said, ''I guess I need a new battle plan.''

''Maybe not a new plan. Just bring out the big guns.''

''How do you mean?''

Patting her cheek, Evie said wisely, "Honey, none of us ever appreciates what we have until we're about to lose it."

Kate thought about it for a long moment. Big guns. Losing what we have. Instantly she thought about General Thornton's letter, still tucked away in her desk. She'd sent a gracious "thanks, but no thanks" letter some time ago, but the general had urged her to think it over. Maybe it was time she did. Maybe it was time to let Thomas know about her offer to work in D.C.

Although, even as she considered it, she thought this new plan sounded like emotional blackmail. But a small voice inside her reminded, *All's fair in love and war.*

"It might not work," she muttered aloud.

"Then you'll be no worse off than you are now."

"True. And if it *does* work…" Just thinking of the possibilities brought a smile to her face. Sometimes, she told herself, a person simply had to take a gamble. Risk everything—no matter how frightening—in an attempt to gain all she'd ever wanted.

Tom walked into the living room and set the videotape down next to three others just like it. For some reason, several of his friends had thought it a hilarious joke to give him copies of the movie, *Father of the Bride, Part Two.*

Personally, he didn't think it was so funny. Every time he watched it, he felt sympathy for the poor man torn between two delivery rooms—one where his grandchild was being born and the other where his own wife was giving birth.

One strange thing, though, he was no longer nervous about entering the parenthood game again. In fact, the past few months had been great. Watching their baby grow inside Kate. Making plans. Reading about the latest changes in childbirth and parenting. He and Jack had even talked about buying the lumber so they could build two cribs themselves.

Tossing his hat onto the nearest chair, Tom unbuttoned his uniform shirt as he turned for the hallway and the bedroom. When he'd gotten married, he would never have believed it would work out this well. But he and Kate had made it work. They'd had some rough spots, true. But on the whole, he thought they'd done a damn fine job of building a marriage based on friendship. Mutual respect. Admiration. Affection.

He smiled to himself at the paleness of that last word. Affection. It didn't come near to defining what he felt around Kate. What it was like to hold her as she fell asleep and kiss her awake in the morning. Couldn't begin to describe the passion they shared that seemed to grow and blossom daily.

He'd even become accustomed to hearing her say, "I love you." More than that, he looked forward to hearing it. He no longer felt guilty about being unable to say the words himself. She seemed to understand that what he felt for her was real and deep and didn't require a label to measure its worth. And for that he was grateful.

"Kate?" he called as he moved down the hall. "Are you home?"

He entered the bedroom and stopped just past the threshold. Kate stood by the wide window, late-afternoon sunshine pouring through the sparkling glass in a molten stream and gilding her hair. Wearing a filmy cotton maternity dress that shifted and swirled about her knees in the breeze, she looked beautiful. Ethereal. Until she half turned to glance at him.

Her expression was at odds with her pose. She seemed so relaxed. So composed. Yet her features were tight, and he could see the evidence of tears long past.

Since her hormones had evened out a couple of months ago, he hadn't seen her shed a single tear. Knowing that she'd been crying now gave him a start.

"Is something wrong?" he asked, a heaviness settling around his heart.

Her hands clasped atop the mound of her belly, her fingers twisted and pulled at each other in an obvious sign of distress. "We have to talk, Thomas."

He'd never known anything good to have come from a conversation starting with those words. Bracing himself for a disaster he couldn't avoid, Tom said simply. "All right. What is it, Kate?"

She took a step away from the window, and the golden nimbus surrounding her darkened before disappearing altogether. "I have to ask you a question, and I want you to think about it carefully before you answer me, okay?"

He nodded stiffly.

Moving closer, Kate stopped when she was standing beside the foot of the bed. Reaching out, she grabbed hold of the footboard and held on with a grip that made her knuckles stand out white against her skin. She took a deep breath, looked him square in the eye and asked, "Do you love me, Thomas?"

Her quiet question hit him with the force of a blow to the solar plexus, robbing him of air, stealing the safe footing he'd thought he was on. He stared at her for a long, silent moment.

"It's a yes-or-no question, Thomas," she said, and her voice sounded far less confident than it had a moment ago.

"Kate, we've been through this before."

"Months ago," she told him quickly.

"Nothing's changed."

"Hasn't it?" She lifted her left hand and placed it atop the swell of their child. "I'm almost eight months pregnant, Thomas. Our child will be born in just a few weeks."

"I know that," he said, and shoved one hand through his hair.

"But you don't know if you love me."

"Kate..."

"Let me finish. Please." She pulled in a shuddering breath, then straightened her spine until she was almost at full attention. "I know I said once that I didn't think I could be a single parent. Heaven knows, it's not the way I would choose to raise my child, but it would be better than raising him in a house without love."

Without love? Friendship was love, wasn't it? They would both love their child, wouldn't they? But he couldn't voice those opinions, because she went right on.

"I was raised like that, Thomas. And I won't do it to my own child. So. If you can't or won't love me, tell me now. I'll request a transfer to Washington right away."

Another blow. "Washington?" he repeated. "You mean General Thornton? That was months ago, Kate. He's probably forgotten he made that offer."

Slowly, her gaze never leaving his, she dipped one hand into a pocket of her dress, pulled out a folded piece of paper and handed it to him. Reaching for it as carefully as he would have, had it been a snake coiled to strike, Tom took the paper and read each line with growing dismay. By the time he'd finished, he felt as though a great, yawning hole had opened up beneath him and he was about to tumble into it.

"How long have you had this?" he asked.

"A few months."

"And you didn't tell me." Betrayal stung him sharply.

"There was no need before," Kate said. "I hadn't any intention of accepting his offer."

"Until now."

She nodded. "Until now."

He folded the letter again and tossed it onto the bed. What could he say? He knew what her career had always meant to her. This was the opportunity of a lifetime.

"So we come back to my question," she said, splintering his thoughts and dragging him back to the moment at hand. "Do you love me, Thomas?"

Damn it, why did it always come back down to this? "I care for you, Kate," he said gruffly. And it was true. He felt more for her than he'd ever believed possible. "I want to be married to you. I want to be a father to my child. Isn't that enough?"

She shook her head slowly, sadly. "Not anymore."

"Why the hell not?" he demanded.

"Because the baby...and I, deserve better. Oh, Thomas. *You* deserve better."

"Haven't we been happy these past few months?" he asked, and heard the note of desperation in his own voice, yet was helpless to contain it.

"Yes," she said, a sad smile curving one corner of her mouth. "We have been. But our future is about to arrive, and Thomas, I want more. For all of us."

She wanted his heart. No strings attached. She wanted his soul, and he wasn't sure he could give it to her. Heck, he wasn't completely sure he still had one.

This time with Kate had been the happiest of his life. He'd wanted it to go on forever, but he should have known it couldn't. She was right. She did deserve more. He didn't—couldn't speak.

And after a silent minute or two passed, Kate said sadly, "I'll contact the general's office tomorrow."

As she walked past him, headed for the doorway, Kate moved slowly, hoping against hope that he would call her back, confess his love and they could live happily ever after.

But he didn't, and when she stopped on the threshold of the guest room to look back at him, her heart sank even further. He hadn't moved an inch. Standing alone in the center of the room, he looked very much what he obviously was. A solitary man who needed no one.

She'd pinned her hopes on this last, all-or-nothing gamble and she'd lost. Stepping into the guest room, she closed the door behind her and gave in to the tears raging inside.

The bed seemed bigger. Colder.

Lonely, dark hours passed, and still he couldn't sleep.

Tom reached out and grabbed the pillow where Kate had laid her head so many nights. Clutching it to his chest, he stared blindly at the moon-washed ceiling above him.

Visions drifted across his mind. Visions of the long, empty years stretching out ahead of him. His imagination conjured up awkward phone calls and uncomfortable visits. His own son would be a stranger to him—just as Donna had been. Once again he would lose the precious few years of childhood.

And Kate. A woman as passionate as she was wouldn't be alone her whole life. Unbidden came mental images of his wife in the arms of some faceless man. A man who wasn't afraid to love. A man who didn't let his past rule his future. A man who could bring himself to say three small words. *I love you.*

The moon dipped behind a bank of clouds, and his bedroom was enveloped by a smothering wall of blackness. When he finally fell asleep, he found no comfort in his dreams. Instead he was haunted by vivid nightmares of Kate and his child, locked away behind walls too high for him to climb.

Kate was up and out of the house before Thomas woke up. She didn't want another confrontation. She didn't want to have to look at him, knowing that he couldn't—or wouldn't—confess his love. Instead she went to her office early, determined to put in a phone call to General Thornton.

It was past time that she began making plans for her and her baby's future. A future that sadly, would not include Thomas.

When he woke up, it was nearly mid-morning and he was alone.

Tom showered, dressed and walked through the empty house to the kitchen. Standing at the counter, he drank a cup of coffee and listened futilely for the sound of Kate's voice coming from another room.

His jaw tight, he realized that the old house seemed to echo with the loneliness that apparently was his destiny. He told himself to get used to the quiet. To welcome the shattering stillness that would forever define his life.

There would be no more quiet moments of shared laughter. No more kisses over morning coffee. No more sweet nights of lovemaking followed by the tenderness of falling asleep with Kate snuggled close to his side.

His gaze shifting around the room, he noticed Kate's jacket hanging on a peg by the back door and her book left on the edge of the table. A pair of her earrings were sitting on the windowsill above the sink. A sale paper on baby furniture had been neatly folded and left near the phone.

She was so much a part of his life, he didn't know how he would survive without her.

Finally his gaze landed on a framed photo of him and Kate together. Taken at a carnival just the month before, they looked happy, smiling into each other's eyes, their hands joined atop their growing child.

Destiny, he thought. Was it really his destiny to live apart from the one woman who had made him feel whole again? Or was destiny what you made of it when you stopped worrying about the future and made a grab for life when it was offered to you?

Straightening up, he set his coffee cup down with a clatter. Better, he thought, to live with the fear of failing at marriage than to face the rest of his life wishing he'd had the courage to love Kate as she deserved to be loved.

Decision made, he raced for the front door, hoping he wasn't too late.

When Thomas burst into her office, Kate was just hanging up the phone.

Slamming her door, he said. 'Was that the general?''

"No," she said, her heartbeat quickening at the sight of him.

"Have you talked to him this morning?"

"Yes,"she answered, noting for the first time that his eyes were shadowed and he looked like a man on the edge. "About two hours ago."

"Call him back," Thomas told her, and reached for her phone, lifting the receiver and holding it out to her. "Damn it, Kate, call him back. Please."

"Why?" she asked. Hope rushed into life inside her, but Kate tried to rein it in, afraid to believe that he meant what she prayed he meant.

He dropped the receiver, came around her desk and grabbed her, pulling her to her feet. Then, cupping her face between his palms, he kissed her, searing her lips and her soul all at once with the desperate passion roaring through him.

"That's why," he said when he lifted his head again. His gaze moved over her hungrily, as though it had been weeks since he'd seen her. "Kate, you married a fool."

"Thomas..."

"Don't stop me now," he warned her with a shake of his head. "It's taken me too long already to say this, and I want to get it said." Stroking her skin with the pads of his thumbs, he whispered. "I love you, Kate." And when the words were finally out, he half laughed to himself. "Wasn't as hard as I thought it would be. I love you. I love you and the baby. Don't leave. Don't go away, when I've just discovered how much you mean to me."

She sucked in a gulp of air, and it shuddered from her in a long sigh. "I want to believe you, Thomas. You don't know how much, but—"

"What?" he asked, terrified now that he *had* come too late to his senses.

"I can't help thinking that the baby is what's

brought this about." She swallowed hard against the bitter taste of the words.

Tom pulled her into the circle of his arms. Holding her tightly, he whispered, "Of course I love the baby, too. He's a part of you. Of me. He's what we made together out of the magic that happens between us. But, Kate—" he drew back, looking deeply into her eyes, willing her to believe him "—I could still be a part of his life if we were apart. It wouldn't be easy, but I could do it. It's *your* life I want to be a part of. Life without you is as empty as that damned house was this morning."

She wanted to believe him. He saw it in her eyes, so he went on, hurriedly, determined to convince her to stay. "I want to be with you. To wake up freezing in the middle of the night to find you've stolen my blankets. To see your face every morning. I want to fight my way through hair dryers, curlers and makeup to get to the bathroom sink."

Her lips twitched even as tears shimmered in her eyes.

"I want to eat burned meat loaf and dry your tears when you cry at those dumb, old movies."

Desperation roared through him. He tried to read the emotion in her eyes, but his own doubts blinded him. Old fears cowered in the dark corners of his soul, snarling and snapping at him, waiting for the chance to tear into him again with enough strength to make him walk away from this one last, best chance for happiness.

But he wouldn't let that happen. Not this time. He wouldn't waste the rest of his life running from a past

long gone. He wouldn't...*couldn't* live without Kate.
"Damn it," he said on a groan, "you're everything
to me. I can't imagine my life without you in it. The
emptiness of that world would kill me. Don't stop
loving me, Kate," he continued in a hoarse whisper.
"Let me love you. Don't leave me. Stay. Stay forever
and then longer. I want to be a part of your life."

Kate let her head fall forward until her forehead
rested on his chest. He kissed the top of her head and
continued in a softer voice. "But mostly, Kate, I just
want to love you. Give me—no. Give *us* another
chance. Call the general and tell him you don't want
the job."

She didn't speak. Fear rose up inside him. Was he
too late? Had he lost her already? No. He wouldn't
give up. "Kate..."

Wrapping her arms around him, Kate hugged him
tightly, then tipped her head back to look up at him.
"I already told him that, when I called him earlier."

"What?" he asked, relishing the sweet pulse of
relief as it beat inside him.

"I realized something myself today, Thomas," she
said. "As important as my career is to me, you and
the baby are *more* important. While I was talking to
the general's adjutant, I decided to stay here and fight
for you. To make you see how much you need me.
How much you love me."

Grinning now, Tom pulled her hard against him,
knowing he would never be able to hold her tightly
enough to suit him. "You know something, Major,"
he whispered, "you're a helluva woman."

"And don't you forget it," she warned, tipping her
head back to welcome his kiss.

Epilogue

One year later

Toys were scattered across the lawn. The summer scent of burning charcoal and barbecuing hamburgers drifted on the ocean breeze. Female laughter rippled toward him from the open kitchen doorway, and from near the grill came Jack's muttered, halfhearted curses as he burned himself. Again.

Tom smiled to himself and looked down at the two babies he held, perched on both of his knees. Angela, Donna and Jack's daughter, gave him a wide, toothless grin as drool rolled down her chin to plop onto his already-wet jeans. A beautiful girl, she made her grandpa proud and her parents completely nuts. Jack and Donna each carried enough photos of Angela in their wallets to stock a moderately sized gallery.

''But then,'' Tom told the baby. ''If you weren't so pretty, they wouldn't bother, would they?''

Angela cooed and shoved his key ring into her mouth.

Tom's gaze shifted to his son and felt his heart swell to monumental proportions. Evan's grin already had two teeth, proving that he wouldn't be outdone by his three-weeks-older niece.

Scooting around on his father's knee, Evan made a try for freedom, and Tom had to laugh. The boy had been on the go practically from the minute he was born. Keeping up with him wouldn't be easy, but Tom was up to it.

He felt younger than he had in years and knew that the blessing of Kate and Evan had been his own personal Fountain of Youth.

''Hey, Jack!'' Donna called from the kitchen, ''Aren't those burgers done yet?''

''Am I the cook today or not?'' Jack called back around the singed finger he'd stuck in his mouth.

Dashing out the back door, Donna went to her husband's side and grunted, ''Man cook. Big fire. Good.''

He gave her a friendly swat on the behind, and she went up on her toes to kiss him.

Tom grinned and silently thanked whatever Fates had granted him this new and precious life. A child. A grandchild. A daughter and son-in-law who were friends as well as family. And, he thought, his gaze shifting to the kitchen doorway where Kate stood smiling at him. Most especially, he was eternally grateful for this woman.

The one woman in the world who made loving so easy.

She jumped off the porch and walked to him, a delicious sway to her hips. When she reached his side, she lifted Evan off his lap and gave the baby a quick, gentle squeeze.

"Are we going to eat today?" she asked, with a look at Jack and the burning burgers.

"Charcoal," he said with a groan and stood up, cradling Angela close. "My favorite," he added, teasing her about her still-less-than-stellar cooking.

"You should be kind to pregnant women," Kate said, and shot him a wicked glance.

"Pregnant?" he repeated, surprised but very pleased. "Are you sure?"

"The doctor just phoned with the results," Kate said, and wiped Evan's chin with her fingertip.

What a difference a year made in a man, he thought. The last time he'd heard those words, he'd panicked. Now he looked forward to ultrasounds, midnight cravings and most especially, he told himself, another living proof of his love for the remarkable woman he'd found.

The ghosts from his past were silent now. As they should be. And his future, with Kate and his family, looked brighter every day. For whatever reason, the Fates had given him another chance, and he thanked God every night that he'd had the strength to reach for that chance and grab it.

Stretching out one arm, he pulled Kate close enough to kiss and when he'd tasted his fill of her—

for the moment—he said lightly, "You know, Kate. I think I've got this daddy thing whipped. What do you say we have twins this time?"

* * * * *

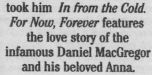

If you enjoyed what you just read,
then we've got an offer you can't resist!

Take 2 bestselling love stories FREE!

Plus get a FREE surprise gift!

Clip this page and mail it to Silhouette Reader Service™

IN U.S.A.	IN CANADA
3010 Walden Ave.	P.O. Box 609
P.O. Box 1867	Fort Erie, Ontario
Buffalo, N.Y. 14240-1867	L2A 5X3

YES! Please send me 2 free Silhouette Desire® novels and my free surprise gift. Then send me 6 brand-new novels every month, which I will receive months before they're available in stores. In the U.S.A., bill me at the bargain price of $3.12 plus 25¢ delivery per book and applicable sales tax, if any*. In Canada, bill me at the bargain price of $3.49 plus 25¢ delivery per book and applicable taxes**. That's the complete price and a savings of over 10% off the cover prices—what a great deal! I understand that accepting the 2 free books and gift places me under no obligation ever to buy any books. I can always return a shipment and cancel at any time. Even if I never buy another book from Silhouette, the 2 free books and gift are mine to keep forever. So why not take us up on our invitation. You'll be glad you did!

225 SEN CNFA
326 SEN CNFC

Name	(PLEASE PRINT)	
Address	Apt.#	
City	State/Prov.	Zip/Postal Code

* Terms and prices subject to change without notice. Sales tax applicable in N.Y.
** Canadian residents will be charged applicable provincial taxes and GST.
   All orders subject to approval. Offer limited to one per household.
   ® are registered trademarks of Harlequin Enterprises Limited.

DES99   ©1998 Harlequin Enterprises Limited

And Baby Makes Three

FIRST TRIMESTER

by

SHERRYL WOODS

Three ornery Adams men are about to be roped
into fatherhood...and they don't suspect a thing!

And Baby Makes Three

APRIL 1999
The phenomenal series
from Sherryl Woods has readers
clamoring for more! And in this special collection,
we discover the stories that started it all....

Luke, Jordan and Cody are tough ranchers set in
their bachelor ways until three beautiful women
beguile them into forsaking their single lives for
instant families. Will each be a match made in
heaven...or the delivery room?

Available at your favorite retail outlet.

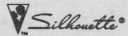

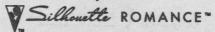

Coming in May 1999

BABY *Fever*

by
New York Times Bestselling Author

KASEY MICHAELS

When three sisters hear their biological
clocks ticking, they know it's
time for action.

But who will they get to father their babies?

Find out how the road to motherhood
leads to love in this brand-new collection.

Available at your favorite retail outlet.

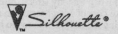

COMING NEXT MONTH

#1213 LOVE ME TRUE—Ann Major
Man of the Month
Why did international film star Joey Fassano ache with longing for a woman he couldn't forget? Heather Wade's parents had finally succeeded in transforming his lovely, free-spirited ex-girlfriend into a cool socialite. But now that Joey knew about Heather's little boy, even her powerful family couldn't keep him from seeing her again....

#1214 THE GROOM'S REVENGE—Susan Crosby
Fortune's Children: The Brides
He was out to destroy the Fortune name! Nothing was going to stop Gray McGuire from avenging his father's death, except maybe beautiful innocent Mollie Shaw. But was exacting his revenge worth the price of losing the love of his life?

#1215 THE COWBOY AND THE VIRGIN—Barbara McMahon
Well-bred Caitlin Delany had no business falling for sexy cowboy Zach Haller, especially since he was a one-night kind of man and she was a virgin! But the irresistible bachelor made her want to throw caution to the wind. And how could Caitlin say no to the man who could just be her Mr. Right?

#1216 HAVING HIS BABY—Beverly Barton
3 Babies for 3 Brothers
When Donna Fields returned from her trip out West, she brought home more than just memories. Nine months later, Jake Bishop was back in town and determined to make a family with Donna and their baby. If only he could convince sweet Donna that even a brooding loner could be a devoted dad—and a loving husband.

#1217 THE SOLITARY SHEIKH—Alexandra Sellers
Sons of the Desert
Prince Omar of Central Barakat was looking for a woman. To be precise, he was looking for someone to tutor his two young daughters. But one look at Jana Stewart and Omar was beginning to believe that *he* was the one in need of a lesson—in love.

#1218 THE BILLIONAIRE'S SECRET BABY—Carol Devine
He had vowed to always watch over his child, even if he had to do it from the shadows. And when tragedy struck, billionaire Jack Tarkenton knew it was time to take care of Meg Masterson and their child himself. Even if it meant marrying the only woman who had the power to bring him to his knees....